Henry James Byron

Partners for Life

An original comedy in three acts

Henry James Byron

Partners for Life
An original comedy in three acts

ISBN/EAN: 9783337064587

Printed in Europe, USA, Canada, Australia, Japan

Cover: Foto ©Andreas Hilbeck / pixelio.de

More available books at **www.hansebooks.com**

PARTNERS FOR LIFE

AN ORIGINAL COMEDY IN THREE ACTS

BY

HENRY J. BYRON

New American Edition, Correctly Reprinted from the Original Authorized Acting Edition, with the Original Cast of the Characters, Synopsis of Incidents, Time of Representation, Description of the Costumes, Scene and Property Plots, Diagrams of the Stage Settings, Sides of Entrance and Exit, Relative Positions of the Performers, Explanation of the Stage Directions, etc., and all of the Stage Business.

NEW YORK
HAROLD ROORBACH
PUBLISHER

PARTNERS FOR LIFE.

CAST OF CHARACTERS.

First performed at the Globe Theatre, London, October 7th, 1871.

Mr. Horace Mervyn (*a country gentleman*).......Mr. David Fisher
Tom Gilroy (*his cousin, at the bar*)...............Mr. H. J. Montague
Muggles (*his confidential servant*).................Mr. H. Compton
Sir Archibald Drelincourt (*a philanthropist*)...Mr. E. W. Garden
Major Billiter (*on half-pay*)........ ....Mr. Flockton
Ernest (*Mervyn's nephew*)........................Mr. C. Sugden
Goppinger (*from the colonies*).....................Mr. A. Tempest
Emily Mervyn (*a young cousin of Mr. Mervyn's*)..Miss F. Josephs
Fanny Smith (*her old schoolfellow*)..............Miss C. Addison
Miss Priscilla (*Mervyn's sister*)..................Miss S. Larkin
Darbyshire (*her maid*)...................... .....Miss Harrison

TIME OF REPRESENTATION—TWO HOURS.

SYNOPSIS OF INCIDENTS.

EMILY MERVYN is whimsical and jealous ; her cousin ERNEST sarcastic and tantalizing. By the capricious will of a deceased uncle, they must marry or forfeit his estate. Though fond of each other they wrangle continually, and are in the midst of a furious quarrel when MR. HORACE MERVYN and his sister, MISS PRISCILLA, appear engaged in a little dispute of their own. MR. MERVYN is a well-preserved elderly gentleman with an ardent fancy for FANNY SMITH, a friend of EMILY'S visiting his house, very positive in manner, but unaccountably under the thumb of his butler MUGGLES, an insolent scoundrel who persecutes his employer by the exercise of some secret power. MISS PRISCILLA, a maiden lady of 46, addicted to parrots and disapproval of FANNY, annoys her brother with derogatory observations about their young guest, when brother and sister are interrupted by the entrance of their cousin TOM GILROY, a rising barrister, likewise the victim of an eccentric will since he cannot marry before a certain age without MERVYN'S consent, except on pain of forfeiting his inheritance. He is followed by MUGGLES with letters for him, among which is an anonymous warning to "keep his eye on Muggles." Then arrive two other guests—DRELINCOURT, a sham philanthropist, and MAJOR BILLITER, a swaggering officer on half pay—both suitors to MISS PRISCILLA, or rather her property. Meanwhile ERNEST and EMILY have excited each other's jealousy, she by expressing interest in GILROY to whom MISS PRISCILLA is secretly attached, he by persistent attentions to FANNY SMITH, whereby he also incurs MERVYN's jealous dislike. Just before dinner is announced, FANNY comes in from a ride and is introduced. But when GILROY is presented to her both are overwhelmed with the surprise of recognition in spite of their attempts to conceal it. MUGGLES makes a note of it, and MISS PRISCILLA, now assured of FANNY's designing ways, resolves to protect dear Tom by hovering around him like a butterfly. The guests depart for dinner, leaving GILROY utterly bewildered at this rencounter with FANNY, who, in fact, is his wife.

GILROY and FANNY SMITH had married five years before, secretly because of the absence of MERVYN's consent to their union. They had quarreled and separated, however, on the former's discovery that his wife had deceived him into believing her penniless, she being in fact a rich girl and he a proud man. Now ensues an absurd chain of cross purposes brought about by the plottings of MUGGLES who hates GILROY and is determined to maintain his mysterious power over MR. MERVYN, whom he worries with certain new and awkward discoveries. GILROY is transfixed with the intelligence that MERVYN is bent upon marrying FANNY ; MERVYN, prompted by MUGGLES. settles upon a match between GILROY and EMILY which arouses ERNEST's jealous fury; EMILY imagines a tenderness between FANNY and GILROY, thereby stirring up MISS PRISCILLA almost to the point of throwing herself into dear Thomas's arms. MISS PRISCILLA sets EMILY by the ears in discovering a bond between FANNY and ERNEST; and FANNY's ire is inflamed by the news of GILROY's impending engagement to EMILY. MAJOR BILLITER, meanwhile, has bribed MUGGLES to deliver a written offer of marriage secretly to MISS PRISCILLA. The explosion comes when ERNEST furiously charges GILROY with undermining EMILY's affections; but this complication is straightened out and the young people's misunderstanding happily adjusted by GILROY's good offices. The latter no sooner establishes his innocence in this quarter, however, than his own wife wrathfully denounces his supposed attachment for EMILY. This precipitates mutual explanation and forgiveness, and the long separated pair come rapturously together, to the utter consternation of the others who appear just in time to witness the reconciliation.

Thwarted and upset in his matrimonial designs, MR. MERVYN is stumped by the collapse of the Kangaroo copper mines and their overwhelming dividends, which misfortune is followed by the failure of the bank in which MISS PRISCILLA's money is invested. He appeals in vain to DRELINCOURT for aid. In this embarrassment MISS PRISCILLA shows the ring of true metal and sets a wholesome example of adapting themselves to circumstances. MUGGLES now suggests MISS SMITH as MERVYN's forlorn hope, but the latter peremptorily refuses to marry the girl for her money. Moreover, some mystery is hinted at which deters MERVYN from any marriage whatever, but causes MUGGLES to urge it with persistence to the end that he may get MERVYN more in his power than ever. Here MAJOR BILLITER comes to offer condolence, but, learning with horror that MISS PRISCILLA is involved in the disaster, promptly bribes MUGGLES to surrender his letter to her, which has not been delivered. ERNEST and EMILY now come in and comfort their cousin with the assurance that they have settled it all and will be married forthwith. At this juncture FANNY SMITH enters equipped for travelling, to take her farewell, it having been intimated that her departure would be appreciated because of the unpleasant circumstance of a few hours before. After expressing sympathy for her host, she scandalizes him with the intelligence that she is a married woman; upsets him with the news that GILROY has secretly married, and suggests that as this was done without MERVYN'S consent, the latter is legally entitled to GILROY'S money and so can retrieve his own misfortunes—a proposition that MERVYN indignantly refuses to entertain. GILROY now comes in, is called to account for marrying without his guardian's consent and concealing the fact, whereupon he questions the latter's conduct in *doing the same.* This precipitates the catastrophe, and one GOPPINGER, just returned from the colonies whither he had been transported formerly on MUGGLES' evidence. It transpires that MERVYN has actually been married but knows not whether his wife be living or dead; that egged on by MUGGLES in a fit of soft-heartedness, years before, he had married GOPPINGER'S wife supposing her to be a maid; that it was the uncertainty about this marriage which had established MUGGLES' long thraldom. To MERVYN'S intense relief his ex-butler is led off under GOPPINGER'S wing in a state of crestfallen collapse, and disappears forever. Then follows the concluding surprise that FANNY SMITH is FANNY GILROY, who, feeling her property a bar to her domestic happiness, has transferred it all to her newly found cousin MERVYN, so that her husband may come back to her without the slightest pang of wounded pride. MERVYN places himself in their hands, all mysteries are cleared away, a general reconciliation ensues, and the GILROYS now assured of future success, commence anew as PARTNERS FOR LIFE.

COSTUMES.

MERVYN.—Short, curly, half-bald gray wig; gray mutton-chop whiskers. Sack coat and trousers of same material; white waistcoat; flower in button-hole. Patent leather shoes.

GILROY.—Black cutaway coat and waistcoat; light trousers; black derby hat.

MUGGLES.—Black suit; white cravat; brown wig, rather long at the back, and brown short side whiskers.

ERNEST.—Tweed sack suit.

DRELINCOURT.—Sandy wig and long side whiskers. Black frock coat; light trousers; white waistcoat; black silk hat.

BILLITER.—Black frock coat buttoned up high; light trousers, with straps; gaiters; black stock; black hat. Short iron-gray bald wig; no beard.

GOPPINGER.—Shabby black suit; soiled collar; black cravat; black hat, the worse for wear. Coat buttoned up close, Sandy hair and beard.

EMILY MERVYN.—Walking costumes. Change for Act III.

FANNY SMITH.—Walking costumes. Change for Act III.

MISS PRISCILLA.—House dresses. Change for Act III. Attractive old maid style.

DARBYSHIRE.—Print dress; linen collar and cuffs; white cap and apron. No jewelry.

PROPERTIES.

ACT I.—Furniture and appointments as per scene-plot. Clock on cabinet up R. C. Flowers in stands. Music on piano and music-rack. L. Parrot in cage, for DARBYSHIRE. Workbasket and colored wools on worktable down R. Three or four letters for MUGGLES. Eyeglasses for TOM. Watch and snuff-box for MERVYN.

ACT II.—Lighted lamp on table behind sofa. Lighted cigarette for TOM. Nosegay for EMILY. Letter and coin for BILLITER.

ACT III.—Furniture as per scene-plot. Busts on bookcases. Writing materials on table. Newspaper and letter for MUGGLES. Lawyers' blue bag for GOPPINGER.

STAGE SETTINGS.

ACTS I. AND II.

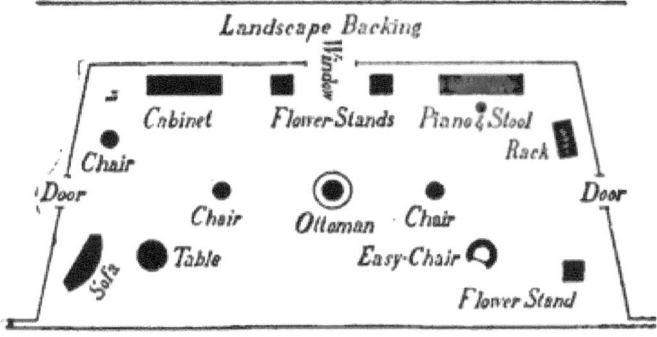

ACT III.

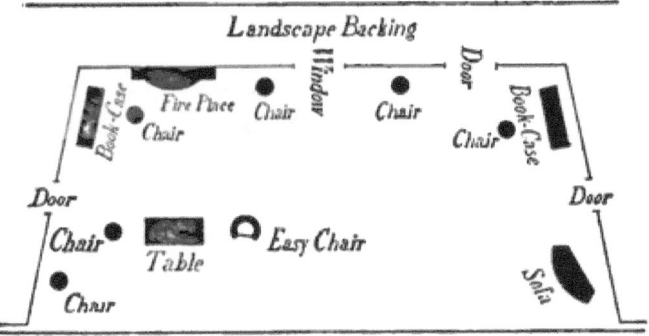

SCENE PLOT.

ACTS I AND II.—Fancy chamber boxed in 3 G., backed with landscape drop in 4 G. Window C. in flat. Doors R. 2 E. and L. 2 E. Piano and stool up L. C. Music rack between piano and door L. Cabinet up R. C. Flower stands between window and piano on one side, and window and cabinet on the other side. Chair R., above door. Ottoman C. Chairs R. C. and L. C. Sofa down R., with small work table in front of it. Flower stand and easy chair down L. Rugs at doors and window. Curtains and cornice at window. Carpet down.

NOTE.—In Act II. the small work table is to be shifted behind the sofa, and a lighted lamp placed upon it.

ACT III.—Library in 3 G., backed with landscape drop in 4 G. Window C., and door L. C. in flat. Doors R. 2 E. and L. 2 E. Fireplace and mantel R. C. in flat. Large library table R. C., with arm chair L. of it. Bookcases up R. and L. Chairs about stage. Sofa down L. Carpet down.

STAGE DIRECTIONS.

The player is supposed to face the audience. R. means right; L., left; C., center; R. C., right of center ; L. C., left of center; D. F., door in the flat or scene running across the back of the stage; R. F., right side of the flat; L. F., left side of the flat; R. D., right door; L. D., left door; C. D., center door; I E., first entrance ; 2 E., second entrance ; U. E., upper entrance; I, 2 or 3 G., first, second or third grooves ; UP STAGE, toward the back; DOWN STAGE, toward the footlights.

R.   R. C.   C.   L. C.   L.

PARTNERS FOR LIFE.

ACT I.

Scene.—*A Drawing-room at a country house.—Window* C. *(with curtains) leading upon a small terrace.—The distant view, a rich country Landscape.—Garden elegantly laid out ; intervening doors* R. *and* L. 2 E. *The room to have something more substantial about its appearance than the conventional " Villa," but still not quite a large " Mansiony " appearance. Ottoman* C.—*Piano and Music stool up* L. C.—*Couch* R.—*Chiffoniers, Chairs, Flower-Stands, &c.*

DARBYSHIRE **enters** *through window* C., *carrying a cage with a parrot in it.*

Darby. (*comes* C.) " Pretty Polly " indeed. You never open your mouth but you tell an untruth. First place you aren't pretty, second place, you arn't a Polly ; leastways, I never heard of the male sex being called a Polly. Ugh ! you ugly wretch, come along to your mistress, *she* appreciates you, and you've had your morning's warm. Ah, *I'd* warm you morning and evening too, if I had *my* way. Come along. (*going towards door* R.)

Enter EMILY MERVYN, C. *from* R.

Emily. (L. C.) Where are you going with the bird, Darbyshire ?

Darby. Well, Miss Priscilla says she feels dull, and would like a little amusement, so she's sent for her parrot, and I'm taking him to her in her room. He's thoroughly warmed through now, she has him put out on the terrace in the sun for a bit every day, until he's regular warmed, miss.

Emily. Put out on the—

Darby. Yes, miss, parrots is like men, miss—generally get warm when they're "put out."

Emily. Don't you try to be clever, Darbyshire, it's dangerous.

Darby La, miss, I don't *try*, it comes natural. Ha! ha! Father was a wag in his way, miss, you know; never succeeded in consequence. He was always funning and always failing. A stupid fellow as took the business after him succeeded wonderful. But, oh, I forgot the parrot: come along, sir.

(**Exit** *with the cage, door* R. 2 E.

Emily. (*apparently out of temper, sits on ottoman, takes off her gloves, hat, &c*). Aunt Priscilla and her parrot indeed! *She's* happy enough; if she *is* forty-six, or *fifty*-six, or whatever it is. Somewhere a long time off. I wonder what *I* shall be like at forty-six, or sixty-four, or whatever the age is. It don't matter much *what* it is, after *thirty*. And what will Ernest look like *then*. Why, bald-headed, and he's too proud to try anything to bring it back. Bah! (*rises petulantly, flings down her hat and crosses to* R. C.)

Enter ERNEST, C. *from* L.

Ernest. (*half chaffing*). Well, have you got over it?

Emily. (*annoyed, in a very quiet voice*). Got over what?

Ernest. (*coming forward, kneeling on ottoman*). Little—em—little *temper* you know.

Emily. (R. C.) Really I—

Ernest. (*quickly*). Just so. Perhaps I was wrong in the term. Let us say *large* temper. There; will that suit you?

Emily. Ernest, I—(*sits on sofa* R.)

Ernest. (*quickly, but with quietude.*) There. Yes, admitted. It does *not* suit you. Fine feathers make fine birds, and the fine plumage of a precious rage don't suit my simple duck, Emily. (*goes to her on sofa*). An ill temper sits very uneasily upon that clear, pale, pretty forehead, Emily; and if you could see the wrinkles that rise only too readily at the command of that vixen vexation; why, you'd think yourself fifty-six if you could only look in the glass.

Emily. (*rising seriously*). I wish I *could* look in the glass, Ernest, I wish I *could*.

Ernest. (*half jestingly*). Well, what's to prevent you. It won't frighten you.

Emily. That's according to who would be looking into it *with* me.

Ernest. (*stealing his arm round her*). Well, if it wasn't Darbyshire, who might be doing your hair, it ought in all consciousness to be *me*.

Emily. (*half nestling towards him*). But you'd rather see another face there than mine.

Ernest. Not Darbyshire's, no.

Emily. What about Miss Smith?

Ernest. *(after a slight pause, releases* EMILY—*rises indignantly, walks to* L.*)* Fanny Smith, good heavens, haven't you dropped *that* yet?

Emily. *(rising)* No; I wish *you* would.

Ernest. *(annoyed).* I! I!

Emily. There! there! Don't keep repeating "*I,*" I'm not *quite* a fool.

Ernest. *(much annoyed).* I don't say you are—*quite.*

Emily. *(laughs a little hysterically).* Ha! ha! how clever— how like a friend—a cousin—a *lover.*

Ernest. *(turning sharply).* A what?

Emily. Oh *I* don't want to tie you down. Go where you please—do *what* you please. Of course our uncles settled we were to be man and wife, and you naturally object to the yoke, very good—*(with a great air of heroism).* I—I release you.

Ernest. *(annoyed, but chaffingly).* Ha! ha! You'd have made a capital actress. I should advise—

Emily. *(now thoroughly enraged).* You wouldn't mind *what* I did. You'd wish me to go out as a governess.

Ernest. Not at all, because you'd inevitably "go in" again.

Emily. Eh?

Ernest. And *not* "win."

Emily. How so, pray?

Ernest. (C.) Governesses have to teach a lot of things. You don't know a lot of things to teach. Governesses have to *put up* with a lot of things. You don't feel disposed to put up with anything. Governesses are obliged to conform to the rules of the house. You are not inclined to conform to anything but that particular whim which takes you at the moment, and which long after that moment, Emily, holds you its merest slave. *(gives the latter part of this with great feeling.)*

Emily. *(hangs her head slightly—short pause).* Perhaps I am wrong, Ernest. I am only a woman—a girl—I may be very foolish, and—

Ernest. *(going to her).* Emily, we are as it were bound together by the capricious will of our uncle which holds over us the one great power, money. I love you; you *know* it. A woman always knows when a man loves her. He has about him two liars—his lips, two truth tellers—his eyes. You *know* I love you, my lips have *told* you so, my eyes have *sworn* it. Had there been great difficulties in the way of our union I should have done all that thew and sinew and a faithful heart could have done to surmount them,—*but,* as fate so wills it, there is no difficulty, everything is plain, straightforward and prosaic, and we (a young romantic pair who think we ought to be separated

by almost impassable **gulfs**, and legal difficulties, and implacable
relations), find on the *contrary* that everything is settled, fixed,
and arranged *for* us. We revolt—only natural—very well.
That being the case, I have no further wish to thwart your
object, which is apparently Major Billiter, or Sir Archibald
Drelincourt.

Emily. *(rising enraged).* What !

Ernest. *(quickly).* Excuse me.   You don't mean "*what,*" you
mean "*which.*"

Emily. *(breathless).* Objects !

Ernest. Certainly ; I consider them *both* "objects."

Emily. Major Billiter—a a—a—

Ernest. *(very quietly).* A major.

Emily. I—I don't even know what a major *is.*

Ernest. Neither I should imagine, does Billiter, but he *is* one
for all that.

Emily. And—and Sir Archibald Drelincourt—

Ernest. Baronet. Come, you know what a baronet is. You
know what a baronet's *wife* is. She's called " my lady," and
she likes it.

Emily. I know you're very cruel. Sir Archibald Drelincourt—

Ernest. Is a philanthropist—a benefactor of the human race.
With him everybody is a man and a brother ; only it's the
younger brother, who gets nothing.   He's the most generous
man in the world, if you take him upon trust, which of course
one *would*, for nobody'd *pay* for him ; though I'm bound to say
he'd let 'em if they offered. He's wonderfully partial to savages
is Sir Archibald—a—at a *distance.* He likes them a long way
off. Savages round the corner in the courts and alleys and un-
wholesome dens he's *not* so partial to.

Emily. He's partial to aunt Priscilla, you know that. So is
the major. *She's* the attraction here.

Ernest. Her money *may* be, not herself. It's a case of " metal
more attractive," especially with the philanthropic one.

(MERVYN'S *and* PRISCILLA'S *voices heard off* R.)

Emily. She's here—you might show *some* sense of propriety I
think, but young men—

Ernest. Are not so immaculate as baronets and majors. *(annoyed, rises and goes up* R. EMILY, *goes up to window.)*

Enter R., MERVYN, *a well-preserved elderly gentleman, and*
MISS PRISCILLA, *an old maid affecting youthful manners.*

Prisc. *(R. C.)* Well you may say what you please. I repeat,
you may say what you please.

Merv. *(L. C.)* No need to repeat it. I always *do.*

Prisc. You *do*, and not invariably in the pleasantest way.

Merv. I'm my own master here, I believe, at least I *try* to be —not always so easy either.

Prisc. Your own master—your butler Muggles is master here. *He* seems to me the chief authority.

Merv. *(annoyed)* Not at all, not at all. Mr. Muggles is an old and attached domestic, and a—a—I presume he always treats you with respect.

Prisc. *(drawing herself up)* Everybody does *that*, Horace, everybody. If *not* it would be—would be—

Merv. Worse for everybody. Just so ; but I must request you *not* to repeat your foolish remarks concerning Miss Smith, a charming young lady who does us the honor to visit us as Emily's friend. You have annoyed me greatly by your observations.

Prisc. My *observation* you mean. I've watched her closely, and I'm correct. I'm perfectly correct.

Merv. Good Heavens ! who **ever** said you were *not?*

Prisc. Don't be coarse, Horace. Miss Smith is **an impostor.** *(sits on sofa* R*., and begins her wool work)*

Merv. Ha ! ha ! has she imposed on *you ?*

Prisc. Nobody **ever** imposes on *me* ; I'm **too deep.**

Merv. *(drily)* You *are*, much.

Prisc. In the first place **she pretends she's** only twenty-three.

Merv. Well she doesn't **look** *that*.

Prisc. Ah, you **men** don't *know* the thousand helps to a youthful appearance women can procure. Why, how old do *I* look ?

Merv. Well—a—don't press me.

Ernest. *(coming down* R. C.*)* You look absurdly young, aunt. Much more youthful than you *are*, you know.

Prisc. This *charming* young lady, as you term her, is not the artless girl you take her for. See how she makes **eyes at our** visitors.

Merv. I'd sooner see her make eyes than *eyebrows*.

Emily. *(up* R. C.*)* Hear ! hear ! uncle. I hate people who **are** always " *making up.*"

Ernest. *(up* L. C.*)* That's true. *Making up* indeed—you prefer continuing *to quarrel*.

Emily. *(at him)* Ugh !

Ernest. *(mocking her)* **Ugh !** *(they persistently* **refuse to** *look at each other.)*

Merv. Priscilla Mervyn, not another word against a lady who is accepting the hospitality of Mervyn House.

Prisc. And whose master is her ardent admirer.

Merv. *(calmly)* Precisely—I am so—I glory in it.

Prisc. Ha ! ha ! he glories in it.

Ernest. *(coming forward* R. C.*)* So do I !

Merv. *(turning)* You !

Emily. (*up* L. C.) Oh, dear, didn't you know that? (*with an air of saying something cutting*). I'm going to meet cousin Tom—dear Tom. How delighted I shall be to see him. He was always *devoted* to *me*.

Ernest. Was he?

Emily. Yes, he was.   (**Exit** C. *and* R.)

Ernest. Phew! Temper, thy name is Emily! Of course we *all*—we *men* at least, admire Miss Smith.

Merv. (*a little annoyed*) You're a *boy*, sir, a stripling. You've no business to admire *anything* but boating and cricket, and a—all that sort of thing. Now, when a man reaches my time of life——

Ernest. (*unabashed*) Why, uncle, I do believe you're a trifle "cut."

Merv. *Cut*, did you say, sir?

Ernest. The least bit *gone*, you know.

Merv. *Cut! Gone!* Hang it, sir, don't speak of your uncle as if he were a cheese. Save your slang for the *ladies—they* don't mind it; I *do;* but then I am, or *hope* I am a gentleman. Times have changed, young man, but in my younger days it was not considered desirable to select one's choicest phrases from the vocabulary of costermongers. (*retires up* L., *dignified*)

Ernest. Very pretty sentiment, but won't bear inspection. You—you know better what was in vogue in *his* younger days, eh, aunt?

Prisc. (*indignant*) Certainly *not*. You forget my age, I think.

Ernest. (*half aside*) Do I? Ha! ha! so do *you*. (EMILY and TOM GILROY *heard talking and laughing*.)

Merv. Ha, here's Tom Gilroy at last; behind his time, but better late than never. (*goes up to meet him*)

Enter TOM GILROY C. *from* R., **with** EMILY *leaning on his arm.*

Merv. (*up* L. C.) How are you, dear boy? welcome!

Tom. (*up* C.) How are you cousin Corney, looking splendid. (*coming forward* R. C.) Ha, Priscilla; no, I must have a cousin's privilege. *kisses her)* Well, Ernest, old man. *(shakes hands with him)*

Ernest. (*up* R. C., *aside biliously*) I wonder if he kissed Emily; she looks as if he had. She's got a sort of "kissed" expression about her.

Prisc. (*down* R., *aside*) What a splendid figure he has. And what a distinguished air. But perhaps he's engaged. (*sighs*) People now rush into matrimony so ridiculously young.

Merv. ('*down* L. C.) Well, Tom, we're delighted to have you amongst us again.

Prisc. (R). That we *are*.

Tom (C). And I'm delighted to be amongst you once more. Why, it's ever so long since I was here. How you're grown Emily, and you too, Ernest, though you mayn't think it. Ah, *you* haven't grown cousin Corney.

Merv. (*uneasily*) No, no—I—a—I **don't** do that sort of thing. (*aside*). All these legal fellows are so personal.

Tom And as for my cousin Priscilla, here—

Merv. Well, hang it, *she* hasn't grown has she **?**

Tom. Yes, she has grown younger than ever, that comes of possessing a good figure. What I always say is, Never mind the face, give me a figure. The latter lasts, whilst features are ephemeral. Anybody staying here ? I know hospitality is your forte.

Merv. Why, yes—that is—(*uneasily*)—only **a** lady—a young lady—**a** friend of Emily's—a Miss Smith.

Tom. (C) Ah. Fine old family the Smiths, only fault **want** concentration, much too broadcast, meet 'em everywhere ; **still** it's a good travelling name. Sort of india-rubber appel- **lation**, like your expanding dressing bag. Take it simply, **S M I T H**, humble, unpretending, respectable, and short. Ties **you to nothing** and envelopes you **in a** cloak of insignificancy **beneath** the folds **of** which nobody cares to peer. Knock out your *I* and substitute *Y*, and you become of another stock, whilst the addition of **a** final *E* really almost removes you into an *aris- tocratic* region. You **may** *then* positively be *somebody*. Shake up the letters and come **out** as Schmidt ; why it's next door but one to a second-hand Bismark. Never *was* such a good name invented. Jones runs it hard, and Brown makes a decent third, but Smith secures the stakes as certain as my name's Gilroy. (*goes up* L. *talks to* ERNEST)

Merv. (*has been staring blankly at* TOM'S *fluency—takes* **a** *pinch of snuff ; aside*). Phew ! He was quite right to go to the bar. (*looks at him*) He's a fine tall fellow, he's taller than *I* **am**. A run-to-seed sort of figure *I* call it, but no doubt I'm pre- judiced. Miss Smith's shortish. Perhaps she'll admire Tom be- cause he's tall. Perhaps he'll admire *her* because she's short. Still, he don't admire *me*, and *I'm* short. Oh, rubbish, he *mustn't* admire her. Besides, ha ! ha ! he can't marry without my con- sent, thanks to eccentric uncle Bernard's will. I've got him under **my** thumb, safe—safe as—Ha, Muggles.

Enter MUGGLES, L. *door with a parcel of letters—he is dressed in black clothes, has a sleeky appearance and hang-dog look he cannot thoroughly disguise—*MERVYN *is uneasy under* MUGGLE'S *glance, and fidgetty in his presence.*

Mug. (*goes to* MERVYN ; *aside to him*). Under your thumb, sir, was you a saying, ha ! ha ! Funny expression that for *you*, sir, ain't it. Letters for Mr. Gilroy. (*goes up to* R. C.)

Tom (*comes down a little, takes them and goes up* R. C., *opening them.*)

Merv. (*aside, a little agitated*). Shall I *ever* be relieved of this persecution ?

Mug. (C., *beside him*) An answer's wanted about that oss.

Merv. (*haughtily*) That *what ?*

Mug. Oss. Oss. You ain't a-going deaf, *are* you, sir ?

Merv. Oh, *horse ?*

Mug. Just so. The *h*introduction of the "haspirit" don't alter the price. Mr. Latimer's coachman and me's old acquaintances—party by the name of Wogg—and whatever Wogg says, *I* swear to.

Merv. And what *does* Wogg say ?

Mug. Wogg says a hundred-and-thirty.

Merv. A hundred-and-thirty pounds for that cream-colored cob !

Mug. Look at the color, so out-of-the-way.

Merv. Out-of-the-way. So's the price.

Mug. *And* its description—Cream Colored Cob—three K's altogether.

Merv. I can't afford it—and I—a—a—I *won't !*

Mug. (*with his finger raised*) Eh !

Merv. (*wincing*) I say I really can*not* afford it.

Mug. But I've given my word of *h*onor to Wogg—I may say I'm *pledged* to Wogg. And though he's a very nice man, and he thinks me the same, I'm afraid if I go off the bargain, he's the sort of party to sink all pussonal feeling and punch my *yead !* Turn it over in your mind—hem ! if there's room. (*they go up* L., *talking*)

Tom. (*up* R. C., *aside to* ERNEST) This is most remarkable and ridiculous. (*reads from letter*) " Keep your eye on Muggles." That's the second time since yesterday, I have received this mysterious piece of advice.

Ernest. (*up* R.) Excellent counsel. He's an awful scoundrel.

Tom. How do you know ?

Ernest. *Don't* know, only I'm certain.

Tom. Quite right. Never bother about reasons, always make up your mind as you *have* done. Saves a world of trouble. (*fixing his glass in his eye, stares hard at* MUGGLES)

Mug. (*to* MERVYN) I say you're wrong, and if *I* say you're wrong, you *are* wrong. There.

Merv. Well, well, well, really I—

Tom. (*up* R. C.) I can't pass my entire time here in keeping my eye on Muggles. Besides, my other eye might object to it, and revenge itself with a chronic squint ; turn against the other in fact ; sort of optical "King's evidence." The small spite of some discharged servant, no doubt ; but I'll *try* my eye on Muggles, notwithstanding. It has had its effect at sessions before *now*, and Muggles may be a scoundrel. Why shouldn't he be ? Most people are. *(looks at* MUGGLES *with a searching glance.)*

Mug. *(in an undertone, almost fiercely, to* MERVYN) I say I've given my word, and if you *don't* buy the oss, I shall look like a—a—*(sees* TOM *surveying him coolly—he quails—tries to continue—breaks down, and slinks off door* L. 2 E.)

Tom. *(aside)* Yes, my anonymous friend, I *will* keep my eye on Muggles.

Enter SERVANT, door L. 2 E.

Serv. *(announces)* Sir Archibald Drelincourt and Major Billiter.

Enter. SIR ARCHIBALD *and the* MAJOR, *door* L. 2 E.—**Exit** SERVANT—*General hand-shaking, and introduction of* TOM— *Then* **exit** MERVYN, *door* L. 2 E.

Ernest. *(down* R. C., *aside maliciously to* EMILY) *Now* you'll be happy.

Emily. *(on sofa* R., *in the same tone)* Oh, I've *been* so ever since dear Tom came.

Ernest. *(scarcely able to contain his annoyance) I* shall go and meet Fanny Smith, she's sure to drive the pony carriage down Ridley's Lane.

Emily. Do, and give my love to her.

Ernest. *(goes up* C., *annoyed)*

Emily. *(rising and going up to him)* And Ernest !—

Ernest. *(turns quickly)* Yes—(MAJOR BILLITER *goes and sits on sofa with* PRISCILLA)

Emily. *(up* L. C.) And your *own* too, if you like.

Ernest. *(scarcely able to master himself)* If you were a *man* I'd talk to you.

Emily. And if *you* were one, I'd talk to *you !*

Ernest. Ah ! *(dashes out* C. *and* R.)

Emily. If I didn't like him so much, I'm sure I should hate him.   (**Exit** *door* L. 2 E.)

Drelin. *(coming forward* L. C., *with* TOM) Oh, yes, Mr. Gilroy I shall count on your co-operation. You legal gentlemen have a knack of placing matters invitingly before a miscellanous audience, and at our meeting you must take the chair—no, pardon me, you *must.*

Tom. (C.) Oh, I'll take everthing you please. But I must confess the object of the society seems a little foggy.

Drelin. Foggy, my dear sir ! What ! populating a territory in Africa which absurd prejudice has declared unhealthy, simply because—

Tom. Simply because everybody dies who goes there.

Drelin. Everybody dies who goes everywhere.

Tom. Unless they come back.

Drelin. We've a surplus population—good—get rid of the surplus population. Send it out wholesale to the banks of the Bangalora river. The idea prevalent here is that it's unhealthy.

Tom. Excuse me. Fatal.

Drelin. Just so. Then my reply is *Pooh!* That's my reply, sir—Pooh!

Tom. Concise, but scarcely convincing.

Drelin. I have a black servant with me, who was *born* on the banks of the Bangalora river ; was reared on the banks of the Bangalora river ; thrived there ; brought up a large family there ; always had his health there. Now mark me—That rash negro *leaves* the banks of the Bangalora river, and seeks those of the Thames, which, the season being winter, and severe—is partially frozen over. What is the result ! (*severely*) That man catches a severe cold on his lungs—he regrets having left his home—he pines—he sinks—and he costs me a pretty doctor's bill. Now Mr. Gilroy, I say that facts are stubborn things, and my expiring black servant says, he considers *Bangalora* healthier than *England*, and as he was *born* there, I think he ought to know.

Prisc. Poor creature, I should like to send him some arrowroot or sago, or something.

Tom. Certainly your anecdote goes to support your theory.

Drelin. Theory ? *Call* it theory if you like, I *believe* in theory.

Tom. I'm a lawyer, and prefer *practice*.

Major. (*who has been talking to* PRISCILLA *on sofa*, R.) By Jove, ma'am, I could have cut him down, the scoundrel ! A low toll-keeper to tell me I'd given him a bad sixpence. If I'd had my sabre, I'd have cut him down. (*rises and goes with* PRISCILLA *on terrace* C.)

Drelin. It's all very well to pooh-pooh these charitable efforts, but I confess I am always thinking of the good of my neighbors.

Tom. For *my* part, from what I know of the good of my neighbors, I confess I *don't* think much of it. I see, Sir Archibald, your philanthropy likes to look a long way off ; *anybody* can see after these poor creatures next door.

Drelin. Just so. I see you understand me.

Tom. Perfectly. Sort of telescopic charity yours, eh? Distance lends enchantment to the view, and that being your view you reciprocate the sentiment by only lending to the *distance*, ha ! ha !

Drelin. Ha ! ha ! Yes, yes. (*they go up* L. C., *laughing and talking*)

Prisc. (*up* C.) Major, doesn't he talk beautifully ?

Major. (*up* R. C.) Hang it, ma'am, he's a Barrister ; spouting's his trade. He's paid for it.

Prisc. Just as you were for killing people.

Major. Ha ! ha ! Just so, and by Jove, ma'am, I earned my money like a man.

Prisc. Ah, Major, you're a terrible person.

Major. So the enemy thought, ma'am, I assure you. (*they come forward* R.)

Enter MERVYN *and* EMILY, *door* L. 2 E.

Merv. (L. C.) Now, Tom, you needn't bother about putting yourself into evening clothes to-day. We're primitive people here, and are consequently polite; no such complete gentleman as your thorough savage—eh, Drelincourt? Ha ! ha !—So we've ordered dinner early, thinking you'd be hungry and tired after your journey. (*looks at his watch*) Jove, it's past the time. (*laughter heard off* R. U. E.) Ha ! *that's* our fair guest, I'll swear to the ring of that laugh.

Prisc. (*down* R., *aside*) So will I—a designing minx.

Enter MISS SMITH *on* ERNEST'S *arm,* C., *from* R. ; *they are laughing and talking.*

Fanny. (*coming down* C.) Oh, how absurd you are, Ernest, how very absurd.

Emily. (L., *aside*) Calls him *Ernest* already. I wish I'd never asked her here.

Fanny. I never enjoyed a drive so much in my life—how those ponies *can* go when they choose, and I *made* them *I* can tell you. Didn't I, Ernest ?

Ernest. (*up* R. C.) You *did.* You managed them like a—like a—

Fanny. Like " anything." Ha ! ha ! *that's* the simile for *me*—means nothing, and everyone understands it. (*crosses to* L. C.) Why, Emily, dear, what's the matter—you look about as cheerful as—what *is* the matter ?

Emily. (*petulantly turning away*) Nothing ! what *should* be ?

Fanny. (*with an expressive raising of the eyebrows*) I hope I've not kept the banquet waiting—my watch is so deceptive.

Merv. (C., *to her with old-fashioned gallantry.*) The watch that could deceive *you* must—

Fanny. (*laughing*) Oh, there, don't pay me any more compliments—flattery runs in the family—Ernest there's been talking the most dreadfully poetical admiration all the way from the gate.

Emily. *(in a great passion which she can scarcely control,
at* ERNEST.) Has he indeed! *(aside)* I don't know which I hate
the most.

Merv. By the way, I must introduce you to my cousin, he's
come down for a day or so. Capital company, talk for ever, and
then begin again. Here my boy. (TOM *comes down* R. C.)
Miss Smith, permit me to introduce my cousin, Mr. Gilroy.

FANNY *has been talking to* EMILY, L.—*Turns, recognizes* TOM
*and starts.—He also starts apparently overwhelmed with
surprise.—Their movements are observed by* PRISCILLA.

Fanny. *(aside)* Tom!
Tom. *(aside)* Fanny, by Jove!

Enter MUGGLES, *door* L. 2 E.

Mug. *(up at door* Dinner is served.
Merv. *up* L. C., *to* FANNY) Permit me. *(offers her his arm,
she takes it mechanically.—they* exeunt, *door* L. 2 E.)
Prisc. (R., *aside*) They know each other. I was certain she
was a " madam." But dear **Tom** shall not be victimized, I will
hover round him like a butterfly, and protect him.
Ernest. *(comes forward, offers* EMILY *his arm.)*
Emily. Certainly *not*. Thank you, Major. *(takes the*
MAJOR'S **arm—they** exeunt, *door* L. 2 E.)
Ernest. *(seizes* DRELINCOURT *by the arm, and drags him off.)*
Tom. *(stands* R. C. *in a state of bewilderment.)*
Prisc. *(sidles up to him.)*
Tom. *(aside)* It can't be! Fanny! *my wife here!*
Prisc. *(trying to attract his attention.)* He-hem!
Tom. *(aside)* What's the meaning of it?
Prisc. (*nudging his elbow)* He-hem! Cousin Thomas. *(he
is absorbed in thought, and takes no notice.)* Dear Thomas.
(vexed.) It seems I must go in to dinner by myself then.
(crossing to door L.)
Mug. Allow me. *(offers his arm—she looks at him indig-
nantly and exit.)*
Tom. *(sinks bewildered on Ottoman.—*MUGGLES *watching
him as)*

ACT DROP DESCENDS RATHER SLOWLY.

————

ACT II.

Scene, *the same as 1st Act.*

Enter MERVYN *and* TOM *from door* L. 2 E.

Merv. *(up* R. C.) Well, now, honestly, Tom—honestly now—
what do you think of her?

Tom. Of her? Of whom?

Merv. Bah! Who *should* I mean but Miss Smith. Fanny— our visitor, Emily's old schoolfellow.

Tom. (L. C.) There can't be two opinions about *her*.

Merv. Certainly not; quite right. Isn't she what you'd call rather a—rather a—

Tom. (*stolidly*). Oh, very much so.

Merv. Hang your cold style of agreeing with a man. I give you some of my very best claret, and the more you absorb, the chillier you become. You lawyer fellows lead such ascetic selfish lives in your rusty old chambers, that there's no rousing you. Living alone's a mistake, sir, and I'm beginning to find it out.

Tom. Well, *you* don't live alone. You can't count Priscilla and Emily as nothing. Then Ernest spends his vacations here, and you seem to keep open house for your neighbors. What more do you want?

Merv. Sympathy—congenial companionship. Ernest and Emily have their own tastes and fancies to follow, and they're not mine. Priscilla—well, Priscilla is—

Tom. Lively company, I'm sure.

Merv. *Too* lively Tom; her friskiness increases with her years. She's as good as gold, and adores me; but a sister's adoration may occasionally lapse into boredom. (*comes forward,* R. C.)

Tom. Ha, how is it you never married years ago?

Merv. (*starting violently—evidently agitated*). What! Eh! What do you mean by that?

Tom. What I say.

Merv. *Mind* what you say, Tom. You barristers have a way of blurting out remarks that—that (*aside*). What the devil am I saying?

Tom. What a remarkable explosion about nothing at all. (*throws away cigarette, and comes forward* L.

Merv. As I was saying, when you interrupted me—my life's dull and colorless. (*sits on ottoman* C). Now, Tom, we're old friends—very old friends—you've been a wild dog, and your uncle Bernard knew it. To prevent you ever making a foolish marriage, you know he left your matrimonial fate in my hands, and you can never marry without my express sanction. If you do, you'll forfeit your little fortune. And I'm an inexorable dog. Ha! ha!

Tom. (*sitting on ottoman*). Uncle Bernard was a confirmed old bachelor, and as such should be pitied, if not despised.

Merv. (*quickly*). That's what *I* say; a man should marry. Even—even if the act should cause him any serious inconvenience, loss or—or—

Tom. (*quickly*). Just so; my sentiments *exactly*.

Merv. Now, though you've been a slap-dash sort of chap, I think highly of your opinion, matured as it has been by experience and knowledge of the world.

Tom. Yes, I've seen a little.

Merv. Just so; and the last thing you've seen—the most recent fact you've noticed—eh. (*playfully tapping him on the chest then sitting back to watch the effect of his words.*)

Tom. (*reflectively*) Well—a—really I can't say—I exactly—

Merv. I observed your eye at dinner; you can't deceive *me;* you never took it off her. You ate nothing—you drank a good deal—the more you took, the more stolid you became—you were *glum,* actually glum. Major Billiter who's next door but one to a chimpanzee at conversation as a *rule,* shone like a Theodore Hook beside you. Tom, you—you have guessed my secret. (*turning aside half bashfully.*)

Tom. (*aside*) I wonder if he's often like this.

Merv. I admit it—I'm not ashamed of it. Thomas, I love her!

Tom. What!

Merv. I love Fanny Smith, as I don't believe any man loved before. (*rises, takes* R.)

Tom. Phew! (*sits back.*)

Merv. (R. C.) It's not surprising, is it?

Tom. A—a little startling at the moment.

Merv. Don't you admire her?

Tom. Immensely.

Merv. Isn't she accomplished?

Tom. Plays and sings, draws and rides, can act charades, and waltz better than any woman in England. (*rises, takes* L.)

Merv. (*astonished*) How do you know that?

Tom. (*a little confused*) Well, I should *fancy* she could. She's a sort of Admirable-Crichtonish appearance, as if she could do anything—(*aside*)—except keep her temper.

Merv. You've hit it exactly. She's simply perfection, and, come now, don't you think she'd make me a delightful wife?

Tom. Well—a—(*aside*) I've gone through a good deal in my day, but this is a *capper* to a career of surprises, and *no* mistake.

Merv. Can you—even *you,* you supercilious rascal you—come, can you find a single objection to her?

Tom. Only one.

Merv. Let's have it, sir, ha! ha! let's have it.

Tom. Well, she's too young.

Merv. Oh, but she'll grow older.

Tom. Yes, so'll *you.*

Merv. (*irritated*) I'm aware of it, sir, I'm aware of it—It requires no ghost from Brick Court Temple, to tell us *that.*

Tom. Why, you're old enough to be her father,—very *much* her father.

Merv. Who said I wasn't, sir ? I'm not ashamed of my age.

Tom. No ; but *she* might be.

Merv. Never mind, sir. Better be an old man's darling, than a young man's slave.

Tom. Very good argument for the old man. I'd sooner be the slave owner myself.

Merv. How can a young woman feel any respect for a stripling only about her own age—or at the best a half a dozen years or so older ? It's these lads who rush into matrimony so young, who find their mistake out, and suffer for it. Now a man at *my* time of life knows his own mind, and—

Tom. Excuse me, doesn't the argument also apply to the woman ? If it *does*, your wife should be a mature lady, who—

Merv. (*in a rage*) I won't *have* a mature lady ; I don't *admire* mature ladies, I like youth, beauty, freshness, girlish innocence, grace, artlessness—damme, sir, don't dictate to *me* about whom I should marry.

Tom. Why not ; You've the power to dictate to *me*. That stupid will—

Merv. Hang it, sir, marry whom you like.

Tom. (*quickly*) Do you mean that ?

Merv. Anybody in the world, sir, except—(*recovering his good humor*). Ha ! ha ! Fanny Smith, my boy. Come, come, don't look so blank. *You* think I ought to marry an old woman, and I prefer to marry a *young* one. Ha ! ha ! that's all. May the difference of a partner never alter cousinship. Ha ! ha ! ha ! (*shakes hands very cordially with* TOM, *and* exit, C. *and* L.)

Tom. In addition to keeping my eye on Muggles, I now have to keep my eye on Mervyn—to say nothing of Fanny, that's three people to two eyes. There's *one* thing certain, he can't marry her. Bigamy's beyond even *her* bold spirit. (*with some feeling*). Besides she can't *quite* have forgotten everything. It's not so *very* long since after all. (*sighs*). Hah ! I wish I could see the conclusion of this case. (**Exit** R. *door—as he does so*)

Enter MUGGLES *slowly, door* l. 2 E., *having been watching, and* MERVYN C. *from* L.—*they meet.*

Merv. (*down* R. C.) Ha, Muggles, you there ?

Mug. (L. C.) The ladies is *h*enjoying of the *h*air, and the Major's a snoring 'ard in the *h*easy chair. As I heer a party with black ringlets and a 'orse pistol say once at the Surry, " Ha ! ha ! we *h*ar *h*alone."

Merv. Muggles !

Mug. The viper have glided off.

Merv. Viper ! Muggles.

Mug. By which term I *denomiate* T. Gilroy, Esquire, Barrister at Lor.

Merv. What do you mean ?

Mug. You must get rid on him. He won't do here ; he's art-
ful and designing, and he'll get round you ; and I ain't a-going
to permit nobody to get round you, whilst *I'm* by.

Merv. Really I—

Mug. It's no good your trying to conceal nothing from *me.*
You're *smit,* that's what *you* are.

Merv. Smit !

Mug. Cupid's taken a *h*aim at your 'art and he's *'it* it. You
was always of a susceptible nature, nobody knows that better
than *me.* Eh, guv'nor ? recollect when we—

Merv. (*in an agony of fear*). Hush ! hush ;

Mug. Ha, them *was* days when, as the poet has it, (*sings
lugubriously.*)

> When we was boys,
> Jolly, jolly boys,
> When we was boys—

Merv. (*in great perturbation*) Oh, hush, pray !

Mug. (*under his breath*) " Together."

Merv. How can you continually torture me by referring to
events of long ago ? Why don't you relieve me of your presence ?
I'll settle anything in reason on you, as I've often told you. You
might set up in business, and be independent in no time.

Mug. Ha, take a public 'ouse. They're obliged to be kep' too
respectable now a days to soot *me.* Your modern licensed
wittler seems to me to pass his time in shuttin' up and gettin'
fined. No ; I prefer servitoode. By going away I might become *my own* master, but in remaining—

Merv. You continue *mine.* Is that it ?

Mug. That's an onpleasant way of puttin' it, but we won't
split *'airs,* Now, you can't gammon a faithful old servant—this
here Mr. Gilroy's fell in love with Miss *Hess.*

Merv. What !

Mug. And you've *h*observed it.

Merv. Certainly not—I saw nothing of the sort.

Mug. Sorry for it. The mole is *not* a domestic *h*animal, and
it's *h*unwise to *h*imitate him in the family *succle.* You ain't
blind nat'rally. *I* watched my friend, and his symptoms is
" spoons."

Merv. (*getting interested*). No, Muggles ; do you really
think so ? (*aside*). Why not ? She'd fascinate anybody. (*to
Mug.*) What proof have you that—

Mug. As a rule, I don't know a more commanding twist than
that Mr. Gilroy have. But to-day ! and after a journey too.
Soup sent away untouched—fish *ditter*—hontrays *do.*—I sus-
pected him over the first course, but when he actually come to

refusing of his *salary*—the temptingest thing as *is*—says I,
"Thomas Gilroy," says I, "you're over 'ed and ears in love with
that young woman," says I, "and all the deeper cos it's sudden
and hinstantaneous."

Merv. Now you mention it, certainly every time I looked at
him, *he*—

Mug. Was a looking at *'er.* Why he *yung* upon her every
syllable. *She* too see the impression she made, and—

Merv. (*fidgetty*) No, no ; do you really think so ?

Mug. Do you suppose every woman don't know when she's
landed another wictim ? Whenever she looked at him it was with
a kind of "*I don't see you*" glance as maddened him, for he bit
at his bread quite *furous* once or twice, and kicked old Billiter
on the shin by accident on purpose, and never begged his pardon. They'll make a match of it, them two.

Merv. (*in a rage*) Never ! Ha, ha ! I've got my young
friend *there* anyhow. If he marries without my leave he's a
pauper.

Mug. Bosh.

Merv. (*turning indignantly*) What, sir !

Mug. Not 'aving any other *h*observation 'andy, I can only
repeat, "*Bosh.*"

Merv. You should be more careful in your remarks.

Mug. So should *you.* What's money to a man like 'im ? Ain't
he making his way at the bar ? Don't he write *h*articles in the
noospapers and *maggerzines ?* Yes, and gets paid for 'em too.
Besides she herself ain't—

Merv. (*softened*) True, true. I beg your pardon, Muggles.
I was carried away by my temper. But what can I do ?

Mug. Make him marry Miss *H*emily, or else kick 'im *h*out.
There you are. There's Muggle's sentiments in a nutshell.

Merv. What ! eh ?

Mug. Verb—sap—a nod's as good as a wink to a blind 'oss.
Somebody's a coming, so I dror in my yorns. If he marries
one, he can't marry *t'other*—*he* ain't likely to run the risk of
big—a———

Merv. (*furiously, starting*) Silence, man ! A subject like
that, you know, is one which—which——

Mug. *Just so.* (*aside*) It's all right ; I've set the train all
reg'lar, and the blow *h*up in the Miller and his Men was a *h*in-
nocent flash compared to the "bust" as is looming in the *future.*

(**Exit** *door* L. 2 E).

Merv. (*alone*) He's right—the scoundrel always is right. I
was a fool to ask Tom down whilst *she* was here—I can't pack
him off. *She* doesn't seem inclined to go, and if she did I couldn't
let her. (*crosses to* L.) *Ernest's* fond of Emily. Pooh ! a boy who

ought to be at school still. It's a bold notion—all that vagabond's are. I—

Enter TOM *and* EMILY, *door* R. 2 E.

Emily. (*comes* C.) Come, Tom, you *were* smitten with her—own it now, like a man. (*places a flower in* TOM'S *buttonhole*).

Tom. (L. C.) Well, have it your own way. Convincing arguments with a pretty girl are like *facts* with a Welsh jury, they rather tell against you.

Emily. Her manners *are* very fascinating at first.

Enter PRISCILLA, *door* R. 2 E.

Tom. Don't the fascination last, then ? Does it wear out like electro gilt, and discover the sham foundation, eh ?

Pris. (L. C.) Some kind of gilt never wears out.

Tom. Ha, that's when one adds *u* to it.

Merv. (*up* L. C.) Ha, ha, ha !

Emily. Ha, ha, ha !

Pris. (*highly annoyed*) I don't see anything humorous about it *myself.* The way Miss Smith goes on is simply offensive. She's got hold of Ernest, and is actually inducing him to *swing* her.

Emily. It's monstrous ! shameful !

Pris. It's really glaring ! (*they go up and look off* C. *and* R.)

Tom. Yes, and it's so soon after dinner.

Merv. (*aside*) I'll do it—I'll strike whilst the iron's hot. I can but fail. Hem. (*comes forward* L. C.) Tom.

Tom. (C.) Yes.

Merv. (*indicating* EMILY) I say, Tom, my boy, she's rather an attractive, fascinating sort of woman, eh ? Eh, Tom ? (*nudging him*).

Tom. (*after looking obtusely*) Which ?

Merv. (*disgusted*) Oh, hang it, save your small jokes for the Old Bailey, or the Bar mess. Which should you choose, you noodle ? Not the *old* one, thank you. Unless you prefer it.

Tom. What do you mean ? (*aside*) I never knew there was lunacy in the family before.

Merv. A man should certainly marry, as you said some time back—a *professional* man especially. Emily's got a pretty little fortune—not *very* much, but a backbone ; and what is a barrister without a backbone ?

Tom. Can't say—I never saw one. At least, not to my knowledge.

Merv. Oh, you know what I mean.

Tom. Yes, yes ; something to *fall back upon.*

Merv. Just so. A fellow with an independence, a certainty—however small—possesses an immeasurable advantage over the mere struggler for his bread.

Tom. But to be dependent for that certainty on one's wife ?

Merv. Go along ! she's fond of you—always was. Her manner shows it. (*pointing to flower in* TOM'S *buttonhole.*)

Tom. (*aside, dismayed*) By George, so it does.

Merv. *I* shan't stand in your way—she's yours.

Tom. But really I—

Merv. Not a word, I insist.

Tom. But I've never said a word that could——

Merv. (*wringing his hand*) *I'll* answer for her—there'll be no difficulty.

Tom. (*aside*) How on earth can I.

Merv. *She's* young—*you* are young.

Tom. (*suddenly*) Ah, that's just it—we're both young.

Merv. All the better. As it ought to be—both of an age, or nearly so—the husband a few years—half-a-dozen or so older, but not more, certainly not *more*.

Emily. (*up at piano* L. C., *looking over music—to* PRIS.) What on earth are they talking so excitedly about ?

Prisc. (*to her*) Let's listen, dear—it's a woman's prerogative. *Talking* and *listening* are conceded to us as our sex's rights ; and after all, when those two privileges are judiciously combined, we want very little else.

Tom. I must say that on reflection your arguments as to the respective ages of husband and wife have thoroughly convinced me. I think with *you* that the man should be the older. *Very much* the older. Remember your own words—" how can a young woman feel any respect for a stripling," etcetera.

Merv. Yes ; but you're *not* a stripling—you're, let me see, you must be quite—

Emily. (*comes forward* L.) What *is* this animated conversation about ?

Merv. (*seizing her hand*) About *you*, my dear—about you and Tom here.

ERNEST *appears* C. *from* L.—*pauses and listens.*

Emily. Me and Tom ?

Merv. Tom's told me all. How is it you've concealed it from me so long, eh ?

Emily. Concealed *what ?*

Ernest. (*up* C. *aside*) What's he saying ?

Tom. (R. C. *aside*) If I were only safe in Brick Court, I'd die happy.

Merv. It's only natural. Emily, Tom loves you, as you know, and I—

Emily. Cousin Tom ! loves me ! Oh, it's some mistake. Isn't it, Tom ?

Tom. (*nervously*) Well, really, I—I— (*aside*) I wonder where my *wife* is?

Pris. (*aside*) I know very little of dear Tom if he cares to link his fortunes with a child like Emily. I could not mistake the meaning of his hurried remark to me just now, that he might ask me to perform a delicate task some day—the look and the pressure of the hand told me all—he loves me.

Merv. Now, sir, here is the dear girl—metaphorically in your arms. Do you reject her? Ask him, Emily. (*pushes her across to* C.)

Emily. (C.) Ask him *what?* (*turns a little, sees* ERNEST *at back.*) There's Ernest listening—how mean of him. But I'll punish my gentleman. (*to* TOM) Dear Cousin Tom, the position in which I find myself is very awkward.

Merv. So it *is*—get closer to him.

Emily. I didn't mean *that*.

Merv. (*irritated*) You don't know *what* you mean. You're too young to know your own mind.

Tom. (*quickly*) That's what *I* say. She's too young—*much* too young to dream of marrying anybody.

Emily. Oh, indeed! I dream of nothing *else*.

Merv. (*to* TOM) There you are. *Dreams* of you—you see.

Ernest. (*aside*) I'll bring this to a head, and pretty quickly too. If he's been talking rubbish to Emily, I'll—I'll—

Pris. (*coming forward* L.) Dear Tom is quite right, Horace; the idea of his marrying Emily! I blush for you.

Merv. (*in a rage*) Go and blush in your own room, then, and don't interfere in what doesn't concern you.

Pris. (*aside*) "What doesn't concern me." (*pressing her hand to her heart*) Quiet, quiet, little flatterer. (*goes up* L.)

Merv. (*to Tom*) Now I'm a man of few words.

Tom. (*aside*) I never knew an inveterate gabbler who didn't always say the same.

Merv. *Very* few—but those few are to the point. I give you both ten minutes.

EMILY *goes up* R.—ERNEST *darts away*.

Emily. } What!
Tom. }

Merv. *Ten* minutes to give me your reply. (*aside*) If he can't settle it all in that time he must be a noodle. (*to* TOM) I'm going to my study; make the most of the time I grant you, and remember I intend to use the power I possess like a tyrant as I am.   (**Exit** *door* L. 2 E.)

Tom. (*crossing to* C. *calling after him*) I say, Bluebeard, listen to reason. (*to* PRIS.) Sister Anne, just intercede, will you.

Emily. (*up* R. *aside*) Ernest's sufferings must be something awful. I can almost hear him writhe.

Pris. (*coming down* L. *of* TOM, *in an undertone*). Thomas.

Tom. (*at back of ottoman, starts*).

Pris. You despise money. So do I. There is a link that binds our sentiments together, and it is *not* a *golden* one. You scorn a marriage for money. So do *I*. Give me a man of intellect—one whose battle-cry is *brains*, not a *banking account*. You are such a man, Thomas, and—well, there, I have said enough, too much perhaps—but you will attribute it to my admiration of your character—so manly, so unselfish, so—a tear or two will flow—excuse me. (*wipes her eyes.*)

Tom. (*aside*) Damn it, here's another of 'em. Well in *this* case I can't say that I'm sorry I *am* married.

Pris. (*taking* TOM'S *hand*) Bless you dearest, Thomas, bless you. (**Exit** *door* L. 2 E., *overcome by her feelings.*)

Tom. (*comes* C.) How shameful to leave me alone with her, really I —(*turns* L. *and finds* ERNEST *pale and determined standing before him.*)

Ernest. (L. C.) You'll excuse me, Mr. Gilroy, but you're a scoundrel.

Tom. (C.) I am not a scoundrel, and I don't excuse you.

Ernest. You're a double dealer, sir.

Tom. I'm not a dealer at all, single or double, I'm a barrister, worse luck. (*laughs.*)

Ernest. What do you mean by undermining Emily's affections ?

Emily. (*coming forward* R. C.) Ridiculous, Ernest ; he's not undermined anything.

Ernest. Of course *you* take his part. But I'll not be made a fool of any longer.

Tom. (*laughing*) Quite right. Then leave off making a fool of yourself.

Ernest. Tom Gilroy, if you were not a relation——

Tom. Oh, waive that and speak out.

Ernest. Then I tell you to your face that I consider your conduct despicable. You are well aware that I love Emily, that Emily loves me.

Emily. Oh, indeed, I like that.

Ernest. You *said* you did, before *he* came.

Emily. (*much hurt*) Go to your Fannys. (*takes* R.)

Tom. (*with a burst of laughter*) His what !

Emily. (R. C.) His Fanny Smiths.

Tom. Ha ! ha ! ha ! this is delicious.

Ernest. (*in a rage*) Laugh away, Mr. Gilroy, your profession makes you heartless. But I'll have *some* revenge. I—I—damme, I'll call you out ! I'll warrant you're a better shot than *I* am, but I'll try your courage anyhow.

Tom. Call out a lawyer ! The thing's an impossibility. Besides, we should have to go to France or Belgium.

Ernest. Then we'll go to both.

Tom. All right. We'll go to France first, and I'll shoot *you;* then off to Belgium where you can shoot me. Anything for a quiet life.

Ernest. (*quickly*) Tom Gilroy, you are turning me into your ridicule.

Tom. (*rather gravely*) Why, of course I am, you silly boy. Now, seriously, do you think I care twopence for Emily ?

Ernest. Eh ?

Tom. Or that she cares a farthing for *me ?*

Ernest. I don't know *what* to think. Everything seems all wrong, and I know *this, I'd*—I'd kill anybody who took her from me.

Emily. (*up to* R. C. *quickly*) Do you mean that, Ernest ?

Ernest. Why, you *know* I do.

Emily. No, I don't ; you've never done it.

Tom. That's because you've never *been* taken from him.

Emily. No, nor never *will* be.

Ernest. (*quickly*) Do *you* mean that ?

Emily. Did I ever tell you an untruth ?

Ernest. Yes ; lots of times.

Tom. Ha ! ha ! ha !

Emily. But I never meant to—you've tortured me enough, I'm sure.

Ernest. Now, I put it to *you*, Tom, do I *look* like a torturer ! (*turns round on his heel*).

Tom. (*looking him up and down*) Certainly not.

Ernest. Very well, then.

Emily. Very well, then.

Tom. It seems to me you're both in rather a fix, and I don't see who's to get you out of it.

Ernest. Why, *you* can, Tom.

Emily. Yes, *you*, dearest Tom.

Ernest. Not "*dearest*," Emily.

Tom. Here, here, *cheapest* if you like—only don't quarrel.

Ernest. Tom, we throw ourselves upon you. (*leans on* TOM'S *left shoulder*)

Emily. Yes, Tom, so we do. (*same business on* TOM'S R. *shoulder*)

Tom. Here, not both together ; it's as much as I can do to support *myself.* Bear up, both of you, I beg. (*throws them off.*)

Ernest. You don't know how devoted I am to Emily here. (*pulls* TOM *by the* L. *arm*)

Emily. And you can't imagine how attached I am to Ernest there. (*pulls* TOM *by the* R. *arm*)

Ernest. There, you hear her, Tom. (*same business*)

Tom. Don't pull me in two. (*they leave go*)

Emily. I've always loved Ernest, and if I *have* occasionally shown a little jealousy or ill-temper, I'm sure I'm punished enough for it *now*. Marry *you*, indeed—I'd as soon marry—I'd as soon marry—

Tom. There, there, don't go into particulars—somebody very awful, no doubt. I'll take my oath I don't want to marry *you*. It's altogether out of my power.

Ernest. Anyway, I'd soon make it so ; I'd—I'd—you should never live to take Emily from me. I'd—

Tom. Blow my brains out of course. The only course you could take which would render it impossible to retaliate.

Ernest. (*vexed*) Oh, you turn everything into a joke.

Emily. (*in same tone*) Yes ; so you *do*, Tom.

Tom. (*laughing*) Confound it, you don't want us all three to begin to *weep*, do you ? "Crier, juncta, in uno." Ha ! ha ! ha !

Ernest. No, Tom, but—but (*with a burst*) Oh, my dear fellow, you don't realize the awful nature of our position. (*takes his* L. *hand*—EMILY *his* R.)

Emily. Reflect, Tom—two young hearts—devoted—beating only for— (*begins to cry*)

Tom. This is affecting, and as you both hold a hand, I can't get at my pocket handkerchief. (*they both let go—going up* C.) Here, let's go and chat the matter out in the open. Come along. (*strolls off* C. *and* R.)

Ernest. (*to* EMILY) Do you think he'll see us through it ?

Emily. If not, we must see *ourselves*. Ernest, I am prepared for the worst—elopement—anything. (*they are going up*)

Ernest. Hang it, do you know what that costs ?

Emily. How *should* I ?

Ernest. It would take a whole year of a fellow's allowance, Emily.

Emily. Oh, you've no courage !

Ernest. Yes, I've lots of courage, but no cash ; and they won't trust us at the Railway Station. (**Exeunt** C. *and* R., *wrangling as they go off.*)

Enter MUGGLES *from door* L. 2 E.—*he watches them off.*

Mug. (R. C.) Pooty creetures. "Sure sich a pair was never seen so justly formed to meet by natur." Hem ! Shakespeare. Never was a young couple so completely cut out for connuberal companionship, but *h*alas ! it "ne'er can be." "Beyold how 'eedless of their fate the little creetures play." Hem ! poet as I can't call to mind at the moment. Ha, here's the Major !

Major (L. C.) By Jove, must have been asleep ever so long—doosid rude of *me.* Hilloa, Muggles.

Mug. Hilloa, Major.

Major. Where's everybody ?

Mug. *H*out in the *h*open *h*air.

Major. Muggles, you and I have always been very good friends. You're a very worthy, respectable person, Mr. Muggles. highly so.

Mug. Hoh! "Praise from Sir Hudibras Stanley is praise indeed !" Hem ! dramatist, name unknown.

Major. I want you to do me a favor.

Mug. Nobody more ready to do anybody a favor than self for —" for a consideration." Hem ! Scotch party who have recently had a centenuary.

Major. (*mysteriously*) You have opportunities of seeing Miss Priscilla Mervyn alone.

Mug. 'Undreds. But as a man of *h*onor, I am bound to say I never avails myself of the privilege.

Major. Do so at the earliest opportunity. Give her this letter.

Mug. (*obtusely*) I don't see it. (*holds out his* L. *hand*)

Major. And accept this sovereign. (*gives him one.*)

Mug. (*taking sovereign and letter*) Ah, I see it now.

Major. You will of course be careful that you are unobserved, Muggles. You understand me ?

Mug. Puffickly.

Major. Just so. " Tral lal lal lar lal lar lar." (*strolls up and off* C. *and* L., *singing.*)

Mug. So old Priscilla's got a *h*offer at last. Good. She's in the way here—interferes with my plans a good deal. Then she's always wanting to see my books. Not that she ever do. (*crosses up* L.)

Fanny. (*crossing to* R. C.) What a relief to get into this nice cool room after the warm love old Mervyn's been making to me. I couldn't get away from him. (MUGGLES *comes down* L. C.) I —(*turns, sees* MUG., *starts.*) Muggles, what a start you gave me. (*sits on ottoman.*)

Mug. Beg pardon, miss, I'm sure. Last thing in the world as I'd do for to startle you, miss. I'm sure if master knew I'd startled *you*, miss, dismissal without warning would be the consequence of sich—

Fanny. Sich, Muggles ?

Mug. Sich condick, miss. Master's express horders is—

" Look after Miss Smith—see as Miss Smith haves all she wants
—mind as her comforts is attended to afore everybody," Ha,
miss, it's something to rouse such sentiments in such a *boosom*
as master's, which, on a hordinary calculation, have panted
these fifty-five year.

Fanny. I'm sure I'm very much indebted to Mr. Mervyn for
his kindness, and to you too, Muggles, for your unremitting
attention.

Mug. Ha, miss, there is some parties as it is 'appiness to
attend on, and *h*others as is gall and wormwood to them as
waits. Sometimes when I'm 'anding Mr. Gilroy his plate at
dinner, I can scarce keep from 'itting 'im 'ard on the yead with
it first, which would nat'rally provoke remark.

Fanny. On *his* part, most probably.   Then you don't like your
master's cousin.   (*aside*). Ha, ha, this is delightful.

Mug. Like him !   Like a party as watches one as if one was a
ticket-of-leave !   However, when he's married to Miss *H*emily—

Fanny. (*rising indignantly*)   What ! married to—

Mug. Don't you know as they're engaged ? At least they're
going to be.   Oh, master's settled all that.

Fanny. Has he though ?

Mug. That'll be the *first* match, and the *second—(grinning
significantly at her.)*

Fanny. (*amused despite her vexation*)   Yours, Muggles?

Mug. Mine ? not by no means. I were born a bachelor, and
I shall continue in the same persuasion.

Fanny. Quite right, Muggles.

Enter TOM C. *from* R.   *He comes down* R. C.

Mug. But, master is another pair of shoes.   You must have
observed—·(*turns his head, catches* TOM'S *eye, and collapses.*)

Tom. (*up* R. C.) I heard your master calling for you a moment ago.

Mug. I fly.   (*goes to door* L., *aside*).   If that fellow's agoing to
upset any of my plans, I'll pison him.   (**Exit,** *door* L.)

Fanny. (R. C.—*with ill-concealed passion*)   So, at last we
meet.

Tom. (*coming left of ottoman*)   At last.

Fanny. And you're engaged, it appears.

Tom. Engaged !   I'm married.

Fanny.   What ?

Tom. I believe our union was a perfectly legal one.   (*sits on
ottoman.*)

Fanny. Yes, indeed.   Worse luck.

Tom. As you say.   Worse luck.

Fanny. For *you ?*

Tom. For *you.*   I thought you intended leaving England.

Fanny. So I did, but something drew me back again. (*looks at him.*)

Tom. And that something?

Fanny. Don't know; a lurking fondness for—

Tom. Yes?

Fanny. My native land.

Tom. Oh. And it's five years since we met.

Fanny. Yes; five long years.

Tom. *Long* years, did you find them?

Fanny. (*quickly*). No, no, *short*. I mean short. (*aside*). He's better looking than ever. (*crosses to* L. C.)

Tom. Lapse of time has not changed the temper, I presume.

Fanny. I should say not in the slightest. But I can't be sure.

Tom. Why?

Fanny. Because I've had no one to try it on since—since we parted.

Tom. Let me see, five years—why, you must be—

Fanny. (*sits in an arm chair* L. C.) Just five years older than when we last met, of course. It's remarkable we should meet like this.

Tom. Ah, is it fate, I wonder?

Fanny. In time to prevent your crime.

Tom. Crime?

Fanny. Marriage with Emily.

Tom. What do you mean? I couldn't.

Fanny. No, but you *would*.

Tom. Hear me swear—

Fanny. No; I heard you once five years ago, that was sufficient.

Tom. Enough to make me. I married you as a penniless girl, and I found you'd deceived me.

Fanny. Found I had money. What a disgrace!

Tom. I felt it so. You knew my position. Up to my eyes in debt with the determination, ay, and the ability to pay off every shilling by my own exertions, and not fling away my wife's money to Oxford harpies and sixty-per-cent. vampires. I never imagined you possessed money.

Fanny. Neither did I—when we married it became *yours*.

Tom. To be dependent upon a wife for money! Why, I could never have looked my own servants in the face with the knowledge that I had to draw their very wages from—from—

Fanny. And yet you actually concealed our marriage from your cousin, because without his consent you could never get your own money. Don't you see the absurdity of the position you take? He happened to be abroad, and—

Tom. And I did not choose to wait, so I married. After a quarrel one day you said—

Fanny. I said what I didn't mean. I said words which if tears could have washed them from one's recollections would have been obliterated long since.

Tom. You told me of my dependent position. You flung your money in my face.

Fanny. Having previously flung it at your feet.

Tom. I didn't choose to stoop and pick it up, Fanny, and I left you, as any man of spirit would have done.

Fanny. And I never asked you to come back, as any woman of spirit would have applauded me for.

Tom. Very true. I have got on *un*assisted, and when I can support a wife—in the style she has a right to expect—

Fanny. (*anxiously*) Yes, Tom, yes—

Tom. Then and then only will I come back humbly—

Fanny. Humbly?

Tom. And ask for a renewal of those ties which *she* alone severed by a deception which—which—

Fanny. And when—supposing such a proposition were entertained by the injured wife—

Tom. Injured!

Fanny. Injured wife; when would your lordship consider it *not* humiliating to acknowledge your lawful spouse?

Tom. (*excitedly*) When I *am* "your lordship," or on the road to it. When I've got my silk gown.

Fanny. (*crosses to* R.) But that may be ever so long. By that time you'll be a grizzly elderly barrister, so taken up with your profession that—

Tom. I shall have no time for the parks, the opera, theatres, concerts, and the numerous other delights without which your existence would be a blank.

Fanny. It's not true. I never go anywhere when Captain Radstock's away.

Tom. (*in a rage, rising*) Captain Radstock—does he take you about?

Fanny. In the absence of my lawful protector, somebody *must*.

Tom. That makes *me* look rather a fool, madam.

Fanny. Very *much* so, indeed, but then he doesn't guess I'm married. (*wickedly*) He *can't*, from the way he goes on. (*crosses to* L.)

Tom. (*almost unable to master his rage*) Oh, indeed—so he "*goes on*," does he! And you consider you're behaving properly in being seen about with—with— (*sits on ottoman again*)

Fanny. (*seated in arm-chair* L.) I would rather lead a domestic life, if I had the opportunity—the pleasant late dinner with the curtains closed and the gas lighted—the music and chat, and the cozy hour or two, with coffee, and one or two of my husband's old friends smoking a cigar and talking of their old bachelor days—the calm pleasant close to the long day ; how charming is the picture if it could but be realized.

Tom. *(aside)* By Jove, how true her words are ! What a waste my life is. What are *my* evenings ? Soda and brandy, and bitter thoughts. Fanny, if such a picture as you have drawn could be--

Fanny. *(with severity)* It could *not.* You yourself broke the chain, it can never be rejoined. It seemed at first formed of the lightest love links, but you soon let me feel you found them fetters. And so you shook them off.

Tom. *(with a burst of affection)* Make me once more a slave, Fanny ; I have suffered more than you can *ever* have done.

Fanny. No, no, my days for making slaves are past. My heart is softer now.

Tom. *(bitterly)* Harder you mean, or you would not let your husband plead for your forgiveness vainly.

Fanny. *(up to him quickly)* And you *do* plead for forgiveness, then ? You do regret the past—you—

Tom. *(with half comic tearfulness)* I want my wife once more. I want to make up for lost years of what might have been a happy companionship, but which has been a bitter lonely life for *me*. *(seizing her hand, and speaking with rapidity and great fervor)* You don't know what it is—after the day's work, worry and excitement—to find yourself in your dull dusty chambers without a living soul to speak to—with no sound audible but the distant roar of the busy streets, and the ticking of the clock upon your mantelpiece, that seems to mock you with its ceaseless " I go on forever " kind of monotony. *(draws her closer to him).* Ah, Fanny, if you could only be a bachelor for a little bit, you'd *pity* me ; pity's akin to love, and you'd forgive me.

Fanny. *(turning to him with great affection)* I do, Tom ; but your cousin—

Tom. Hang all the cousins in the universe. You're mine once more, darling ; nothing shall ever separate us.

Fanny. Nothing, Tom, nothing !

Tom. We're partners once again.

Fanny. Yes, yes, and *this* time—

Tom. Partners for life ! *(rapturously embraces her.)*

*Simultaneously—***Enter** Mervyn C. *from* L.—Emily *and* Ernest C. *from* R.—Priscilla *from* L. *door, followed by* Muggles.— Mervyn *throws up his hands in astonishment, up* L. C.— Priscilla *shrieks and falls into the arms of* Muggles, L.— Emily *covers her eyes with her hands,* Ernest *beside her, up* R. C.

Tableau.

ACT DROP, NOT TOO QUICK.

ACT III.

Scene.—*Library and study at* Mr. Mervyn's—*Bookcases with books.—Busts over them.—Handsome fireplace up* R. C.—*Doors* R. *and* L. 2 E.— *Window* C., *showing landscape through. —Door up* I. C.—*Turkey Carpet.—Rich furniture of carved oak, covered with scarlet or green velvet.—A large library table* R. C.—*Easy chair* L. *of table.—Pens, ink, paper, ruler, &c., all on table.—Couch* L.—*Chairs about stage.*

Mervyn *is walking to and fro excitedly.* Sir Archibald Drelincourt *seated* L. *of table.*

Sir A. Really it is very sad, very sad indeed, my dear friend.

Merv. Sad ! *Sad !* Sir Archibald Drelincourt. "Sad " is not the word. Not the word at all.

Sir A. Well, we'll say "distressing."

Merv. Oh, *distressing* doesn't meet the case. Doesn't come anywhere near it.

Sir A. Well, "maddening" then.

Merv. Ah, *maddening's* nearer the mark if you like. Yes, it is maddening. And it's always paid such an enormous percentage—such an overwhelming percentage.

Sir A. Overwhelming percentages soon wear themselves out. I find the consols quite good enough for *me*. Those, with a few foreign securities that I can rely on, suffice for my humble wants, and enable me to subscribe my occasional mite—I say it advisedly—*mite*—to those distant objects of charity, concerning which I have so often spoken to you.

Merv. Misfortunes never come singly. Thwarted and upset as I was already, here comes this terrible news. If the Kangaroo copper mines *have* collapsed I'm—I'm—damme, I'm stumped, Drelincourt. There is only one word for my position, and that is *stumped*, sir. (*crosses up to* L. C.)

Sir A. (*shrugging his shoulders*) Ha—ah ! Unwise investment—very. And the panic is almost certain to smash up Hopkinsons.

Merv. (*starting*) You don't tell me *that !* Why man, I relied on Hopkinsons as I would have done on the Bank of England. I wouldn't—

Enter Muggles *suddenly from door* L. 2 E., *with an "Echo" newspaper.*

Mug. (L.) Pretty noos. Hopkinsons put up their shutters.

Merv. (*sinks on chair up* L. C.) Talk of the devil !—

Mug. That's old Dan'l Hopkinson. Leastways everybody says so. He's been living on a wolcanium all these years, and now as there's a regler 'ruption, he's packed up all as he could lay 'old of and *h*eloped to Spain. Second *h*edition of the *Hekker*. (*gives it to* MERVYN.) How they can sell you such a lot of bad noos for a 'apenny is astonishing.

Merv. This is a double blow, indeed.

Mug. (*aside*) One, two—buckle my shoe. Hem ! Poet as devotes hisself to the nussery.

Merv. (*rises, takes* R. *corner ; aside*) And Priscilla's money was invested there—what—what shall I do ? Muggles, leave us.

Mug. Suttingly. (*aside*). He's agoing to ask the Bart to assist him. Vain 'ope. Catch a phi-lan-*thro*-phist assisting of anybody unless it's *hisself*. (Exit *door* L. 2 E.)

Merv. (*up to table* R. C.) Drelincourt, I never asked a favor of any man before in my life, but this dreadful business has thrown me as it were on my beam ends. I have one or two important payments to make early in the month, and—and—in short, can you assist me ? Be assured I shall never forget the obligation, and when I've had time to turn myself round—

Sir A. (*putting on his gloves, demurely*) Mervyn, my friend, my *dear* friend—

Merv. Your *old* friend. (*offers his hand*)

Sir A. My "*old-enough-to-know-better*" friend. I make a point of never assisting neighbors. The system's a bad one—a very bad one. Were you on the banks of the Bangalora river—

Merv. Oh, damn the Bangalora river. (*sits* R. *of table*)

Sir A. (*very quietly*) They have *endeavored* to do so, but in vain. Irrigation, drainage, and the water system generally, is at present in its infancy in *that* neglected clime. But pumps and perseverance may yet do much.

Merv. You can answer for the pumps, no doubt.

Sir A. (*rising*) Mr. Mervyn, your behavior is uncalled for, your jest is obscure, and your general tone offensive. If you have lost your money, you might keep your temper. Learn philosophy, my dear sir. Remember, we are born to suffer.

Merv. (*in a rage*) You'll remember it if you don't get out.

Sir A. (*drawing himself up*) Get out, sir ! Are you mad or intoxicated ! *You're* not the only person in the world who has suffered misfortunes. Look at the pigs I lost last winter ; remember how the hail storm beat down my best field of wheat the year before, and a cow worth twenty pounds choked herself under my very nose with a turnip. Did *I* go about insulting my neighbors ? Did *I* tell people to get out ? No, sir, I trust that in a more resigned and meeker spirit I—

Merv. (*calls*) Muggles !

Enter MUGGLES *sharply from door* L. 2 E.

Oh, you're there, eh.

Mug. (L. C.) Thought it best to be as near the key-hole—I mean the door—as possible.

Merv. (*rises*) Show Sir Archibald Drelincourt out.

Sir A. (*in a rage*) It serves me right for—for ever associating with such *canaille*.   (**Exit** *door* L. 2 E.)

Mug. 'Ere, are you going to stand being called a canal? It's only another way of cutting you.

Merv. Rubbish! he means I'm low, vulgar.

Mug. Don't see as that's any excuse myself.

(**Exit** *door* L. 2 E.)

Merv. There's a type of what I may expect. (*coming forward* C.) What's to be done? (*goes up* L.*of table*) What's to be done? *sinks into chair* L. *of table.*)

Enter PRISCILLA *from door up* L. C.

Pris. (*leaning over his shoulder*) Horace, dear, what's this dreadful news? is it true?

Merv. Dreadful news is *always* true; it's only good news there's ever any doubt about. I'm next but one to ruined, my dear.

Pris. But there's my money.

Merv. My dear sister don't you know we both rowed in the same boat? Your money has gone with mine, and we're little better than a couple of paupers. What's to be done?

Pris. (*with a sudden courage*) Well, brother, the first thing we must do is to *bear up*, the *last* thing to *give way*. People have lost their money before *us*. We're not the first folks who have had to rough it—and let us thank heaven that we've health and strength *to* rough it, that *your* hat and *my* bonnet cover our families, and (*taking his hand*) we'll go hand in hand through life the best of friends, and in the best of spirits, if we must give up the luxuries we never wanted, and learn to prize the simpler pleasures of a humbler but a no less happy life. (*they hold each other's hands.*)

Merv. You're a true woman, Priscilla, old girl, a good woman, and I'll try my hardest to follow your bright example—if I can.

Pris. (*goes to fireplace up* R. C. *crying*) Of course there'll be a sale.

Merv. (*in horror*) A what?

Pris. Gracious, man, don't be absurd. A sale—stair carpet out of the drawing-room window, catalogues of "superior modern furniture," dreadful men with husky voices on the doorstep, and every old maid in the neighborhood collected on forms and making believe to bid.

Merv. (*aside*) How detestably graphic she is.

Pris. The furniture's excellent and will fetch a long sum. (*coming forward a little*) Why, my parrot's good for a ten pound note.

Merv. A ten pound—

Pris. Certainly. Look at the low language he uses.

Merv. Ha ! I forgot that.

Pris. *He* hasn't, though. Bless his old beak. (*goes up to mantelpiece again*) We'll take a nice cheap little cottage. Ernest must go into a merchant's office, and Emily—

Enter MUGGLES *from door* L. 2 E.

Merv. What's to become of Muggles ?

Mug. *Percisely.* What's to become of Muggles ?

Pris. (*indignantly*) Why, of course he will go away and look for another situation, and endeavor to do his duty—(*moving towards door up* L. C.)—and keep his place. (**Exit** *door up* L. C. MERVYN *rises, gets round and sits* R. *of table.*)

Mug. (*smiling pityingly, aside*) She means well. She's a hiritating old gal, but she *means* well. " Keep his place." Yes, he *means* to. Well, sir and how do you feel now ? Do you see your course at all ? Eh !

Merv. Beyond giving up all I can, and endeavoring by retrenchment, rigid economy, and the greatest—

Mug. Bah ! Don't talk copy books, 'cos my eddication having been neglected, texts is troublesome. Don't you see your game ?

Merv. My game ?

Mug. Miss Smith.

Merv. (*rises, violently*) Be silent, sir, you know how I admired that young lady. That—that—I was most anxious to make her mistress of Mervyn Hall—but remember the position in which—which—(*comes* R. C.) No, Muggles, I believe and hope her boxes are being packed preparatory to her departure from a house which she has—she has—(*goes up a little.*)

Mug. Which she's *what?* Now look at the affair sensible. It seems as your cousin Mr. Gilroy and her have met before,— is in fact, old acquaintances. Very good. They meets at the 'ouse of a mutual friend. Carried away by the *h*eloquency of the legal party, the lady reclines for a moment in his arms. *H*unfortunately, (and the same thing 'ave 'appened to myself) other parties arrive at the *critickle* moment. Result.—General explosion. But very big explosions often *h*arises from a remarkable small amount of powder.

Merv. (R. C.) Muggles, occupying a humble sphere, you have stopped short of being a clever scoundrel ; with a further field and larger opportunities you might have turned out a hero. Your arguments are quite unanswerable, and so—

Mug. And so you're agoing to try and answer 'em ; I never knew nobody as didn't do the same thing. Now listen to reason. She's got money—got a lot of money—and it's at her own disposal.

Merv. How can you be sure of that ?

Mug. Bless your 'art, leave us servants alone for twigging parties with long purses. There's a sort of *h*electricity about 'em as communicates *d*irect to the servants' 'all. When one of your rich city friends comes to see you, do you think we don't sum him up on the spot ? The very *h*accents of his voice says "tin." There's ready money in the curl of his lip, and *h*independence in his *h*i. As you pass behind him a-waiting at dinner, 'is very *yair roil* is red*o*lient of property. As for them young clerks and seedy old swells as you 'ave down sometimes as "nll-ups," the very way they wipes their boots on the yall *mat* speaks wolumes. Miss Smith mayn't be a million*aire*, nor yet a million*airess*, and though the situation with Mr. Gilroy were equi*vo-kial*, she's your only chance—your forlorn 'ope.

Merv. But all this is guess-work—mere surmise. You have really no proof that—

Mug. I see her last Toosday a sittin' and writin' cheques by *yolesale*.

Merv. No, no, it can't be. I wouldn't marry a woman of my *own* age for money ; still less would I this girl who—who— (*with intensity*) Besides you know that I—I—. Muggles, you know the mystery that—that—

Mug. (*densely*) I know *nothing*. I remember nothing. The facts of the past have vanished from the memory of Muggles.

Merv. No pretence, no sham, no *lies*, Muggles—you forget *nothing*, and you have taken ample and *cruel* care that *I* should forget nothing as *well*. (*in grief*.)

Mug. (*still obtusely*) I've forgotten what *ought* to be forgotten, and I'm not agoing to remember it again if I don't *choose !* As the witness, when he was accused of having a bad memory, said to the judge, " It's not me, recorder." Why you should always be *yarping* on the one string, I can't make out. You paid a certain sum to get rid of a certain annoyance—and you ain't *been* annoyed, have you ?

Merv. But don't you see, man, that if she were proved to be living *still*, I should simply—

Mug. No, I don't—I don't see nothing, and I won't—

Merv. I must write at once to Atkins and Jones. (*goes and sits* R. *of table*) Something must be done instantly—my head swims and my hand shakes so, I can scarcely—(*begins writing nervously.*)

Mug. (*aside*) Once married to Miss Hess, and he's more under my thumb than ever. That's one way out of the yole.

Then there's the Major's proposal to the old lady. (*with contempt*) Bah ! 'arf pay—'arf pay, not worth fighting for. Don't seem to care for a smash and a sell-up, though. Hang speckelation—whenever he does anything without consulting *me* it's always a mull.

MAJOR BILLITER *bursts in, door* L. 2 E.

Major. (*crossing to* L. *of table*) What's this I hear ? Can't be true, Mervyn, my dear fellow. Met Drelincourt rushing down the avenue declaring you'd lost your money and your wits at the same time.

Merv. Quite true as regards the former. Don't pity me, Major, I'm too cut up to stand sympathy. (*goes on writing*)

Major. (*comes* C. *to* MUGGLES) Muggles, what's it all mean ?

Mug. It means the panic 'ave *h*added two fresh victims to its carpacious *mor*.

Major. *Two* ! *Two* victims !

Mug. Brother and sister. Master and Miss Priscilla. Miss Priscilla in partickler.

Major. Impossible !

Mug. Quite so. Still it's a fact.

Major. But I always understood—

Mug. You always understood as Hopkinsons was reg'lar rocks. But when *h*earthquakes comes sudden, rocks is apt to suffer.

Major. (*in horror, half aside*) Why, confound it, I—

Mug. (*quietly*) You *did*, and there's no getting out of it.

Major. (*blusteringly*) What do you mean, sir ? How dare you !

Mug. (*shaking his finger at him*) Look here, Major, the governor there's a writing a letter, and it's rude to 'oller. Any further *h*observations you may feel disposed to make, please make 'em " *Sutty vochey.*" Hem ! Forrin hauthor.

Major. (*aside*). The scoundrel's right. I must manœuvre. (*to* MUGGLES *in undertones*). You remember that note I gave you some time back.

Mug. It wasn't a note. It was only a sovereign.

Major. Pshaw ! a letter. I must have it *back*, Muggles.

Mug. What, the sovereign ?

Major. No, the—the—

Mug. The billy doo ?

Major. Nothing of the kind, sir. A mere business communication, but I particularly require its return. I'll give you another sovereign if you can—

Mug. Look here, Major, as I am powerful I'll be mussiful. You're on the magistrate's bench here, with authority—your word's *lor*, and precious rum lor it often *is*. Now if ever I apply for a license for the " Dog and Duck," you'll see as it ain't refused ?

Major. I'm afraid the notorious character of the place will prevent my—

Mug. (*going* L). Then I *must* see as she gets that letter.

Major. Here! Here! Consider the " Dog and Duck " licensed. I promise ; and *my* word—a soldier's word—

Mug. There's the *doky*ment, and it's a bargain. (*gives him letter.*)

Major. (*aside*). What a relief ! (*goes up* R. C. *to* MERVYN). Mervyn, my dear fellow, you must bear up. There's my hand. Anything an old campaigner can do for you at any time, command—command. I've had losses myself—devilish heavy ones, but I whistled away my sorrows, sir. You do the same, and all's sure to come right in the end. Exit, *door* L. 2 E., *singing*. " When the heart of a man is oppressed with care," *etc.* MERVYN *sits dejected, with his head resting on his hand.*)

Mug. (*in smiling admiration of the* MAJOR) " How happy the soldier what lives on his pay. And something or other a shilling a day." Hem ! Military poet—partially forgotten. (*goes up* C. *looking through window*). He don't feel misfortunes, not 'im. He's the sort of—oh, Law ! (*apparently sees something alarming, which causes him to start violently ; he staggers down to back of table, and lets his hands fall heavily on it, quite overcome.*)

Merv. (*startled, rises nervously*) What the deuce is the matter, man ! My nerves are sufficiently upset already without —without—(*quite upset, sits again.*)

Mug. (*with his hand to his heart going* C. *to* L.) Down, down, perturbed spirit. Phew ! (*to* MERV.) Other parties has nerves as well as *you.* (*aside*). I could have sworn it was—it was —pah ! But that's impossible. *He's* booked safe enough, and likenesses *do* appear in the best reggle-ated back gardens. (ERNEST *and* EMILY *have entered from door* L. 2 E., *unperceived.* —EMILY *goes behind* MERVYN'S *table, and places her arm round his neck ; at the same moment* ERNEST L. *of* MUGGLES, *coughs.* MERVYN *starts slightly,* MUGGLES *violently, his nerves being evidently upset.*)

Emily. (*at back of table*) *Dear* Cousin Horace.

Mug. (*aside*) Railly, these sudden shocks should be considered in a party's wages.

Ernest. Muggles.

Mug. Yes, Mr. Hernest.

Ernest. We wish to be *alone* with your master.

Mug. Suttinly, sir. (*going towards door* L., *aside*) Well, it *were* a remarkable likeness, it were a—

(*catches* ERNEST'S *eye, and* exit *door* L. 2 E.

Emily. Ernest and I have settled it all, dear, and cousin Priscilla says she's charmed with it ; the notion's splendid.

Merv. What notion, dear ?

Ernest. (L. *of table*) Well, in the first place we're going to get married.

Merv. Marry your aunt ? you can't do it.

Ernest. No, Emily and me. She's got an income. I'll *show* you what the education you have helped me to will result in. Lord Rockleigh, my old college friend, will give me three hundred a year as secretary to-morrow, and jump at it, and we'll all live together, a downright happy family, Uncle Horace. (*places his arm round* EMILY'S *waist*)

Merv. My dear boy, you speak impossibilities.

Emily. Oh, but it's settled. We've as good as taken the house, haven't we, Ernest ?

Ernest. Better.

Emily. But before we do *anything*, we're going to make conditions, Horace dear. You must tell him, Ernest.

Ernest. You must shake hands with Tom.

Emily. And forgive him.

Merv. (*rises, crosses to* L. EMILY *comes down* R. ERNEST *comes* C.) Never ! Don't misjudge me. It is *not* from any foolish jealous feeling ; my short silly dream is at an end, and I blush now at my own conceit and selfishness. That young lady's hold over my soft old heart has lost its power. But Tom—my old friend and relative, to *know* what he must have done, and yet permit me to—to—

Emily. (*crossing to* C.) But don't you see that's just what he didn't do. He tried his best to argue you out of proposing to her, and was too much a gentleman, no doubt, to state his reasons. It now seems they were old acquaintances, and probably his knowledge of her prompted the advice he gave you.

Merv. By Jove, Emily, that's true. (*takes* L. *corner*) I see the force of the—

FANNY SMITH *appears at door up* L. C., *dressed for travelling.*

Fanny. (*meekly*) May I come in ? (*comes down* C., *they all three appear very uncomfortable*)

Emily. (R. C. ; *after a slight pause, at* FANNY) The carriage is ordered, I believe, Ernest ?

Ernest. (R.) I have given instructions.

Fanny. (L. C., *aside*) Poor things, I'm not surprised—it's only natural. (*to* MERVYN) Mr. Mervyn, notwithstanding the painful position in which you beheld me a few hours since—

Emily. (*aside*) Indeed ! There didn't seem to be much *pain* about it.

Merv. (*loftily*) Pray, madam, do not allude to that unpleasant circumstance.

Fanny. I wish to say good-bye before going—to shake you by the hand—to say a word or two of sympathy, however unwelcome they may prove—for I have heard, believe me, with sincere grief, of the sudden heavy loss you—(*is overcome*)

Merv. (*blowing his nose, a little moved ; aside*) If she cries. I'm done for.

Ernest. (*aside to* EMILY) She really appears cut up.

Emily. Cut up ! Ha ! *The crocodile.*

Fanny. (*to* MERV.) I have a few remarks to make to you, which—

Emily. (*coldly*) Pray, make them.

Fanny. Which are for your private ear.

Emily. (*huffed*) Ho ! indeed !

Ernest. (*to* EMILY) We'd better clear out. She *can* do no further harm.

Emily. (*going to door* R.) Oh, certainly. (*to* ERNEST) And you could admire that woman ! (**Exit** *in a restrained rage, door* R. 2 E.)

Ernest. I wish I could be mean enough to listen. (**Exit** *door* R. 2 E.)

Merv. (*crossing in front to* R., *indicating easy chair* L. *of table*) Pray be seated. (FANNY *goes up and sits* L. *of table.* MERV. *sits* R. *of table, fidgetty, the more so from her self-possession*)

Fanny. (*with perfect composure*) Mr. Mervyn, in ten minutes or so I leave your hospitable roof—

Merv. Mine no longer.

Fanny. Don't interrupt me——

Merv. Madam !

Fanny. If you please. I am sorry to go away—leaving a bad impression, and Emily I will *never* forgive.

Merv. Eh ?

Fanny. Until she asks *my* forgiveness.

Merv. That she will—

Fanny. (*quickly*) Do before long. However, as regards my being discovered—let us speak out and call a spade a spade—almost embracing—

Merv. (*quickly*) Quite. Quite.

Fanny. Just so. Mr. Gilroy. That naturally aroused your indignation, your *jealous* indignation.

Merv. Jealous !

Fanny. You admired me. You would have wished to make me Mrs. Mervyn, but—(*very markedly*)—that you could *not do.*

Merv. (*jumps up sharply, much agitated*). How do you know *that,* madam ? How do you know that ? Who has been talking to you about my affairs ? Who has dared to—to—

Fanny. Nobody. What's the matter ? I was only going to say it would be an impossibility, because—

Merv. (*painfully agitated*) Because—

Fanny. Because I happen to possess a husband already.

Merv. *You ! you* possess a—(*sinks into chair, relieved*). I breathe once more. I thought you were going to say that *I*— Phew !

Fanny. Yes, Mr. Mervyn, I'm a married woman.

Merv. (*rises, speaks across the table*) Oh, indeed. And you actually, positively bring that fact forward as an excuse for your behavior. Don't you see it aggravates it, madam? (*comes down front, then back again*). But there, there, I've no right to talk to you like this ; the carriage will soon be ready, and—excuse me, my time is valuable, and this sudden change in our fortunes necessitates my—(*sits again*)

Fanny. Listening to reason. Listening to a friend whom you may find where you least expect it.

Merv. (*bitterly*) Ha ! ha ! Yes, it will certainly be *there.*

Fanny. I know something of your family arrangements.

Merv. (*again alarmed*). *You do ?* You'll excuse me, but—

Fanny. (*with authority*). You'll excuse *me,* but I shall be obliged if you will hear me out without interruption. You've come to grief.

Merv. Well, it's come to *me.*

Fanny. Same thing. You had an eccentric relative, I believe, who left a strange will to the effect that if his rather wild nephew, Mr. Gilroy, married against your consent before the age of thirty-five, his very considerable legacy was to go to *you.*

Merv. Quite true. Bernard was half mad, only it doesn't do to say so.

Fanny. Suppose he *should* marry without your consent.

Merv. He knows better.

Fanny. Don't make so sure of that.

Merv. My dear madam, I make sure of nothing for the future. I made sure of the stability of Hopkinsons'—I made sure of the big profits from the Kangaroo mine—I made sure of Tom's good faith, of Drelincourt's friendship, of your simplicity, of—of— Bah ! everything's false and bad, and—

Fanny. Suppose he—a—he *has* married ?

Merv. What !

Fanny. People *do* marry sometimes, and conceal the fact for years.

Merv. (*rising quickly, again bursting out*). Madam ! I don't know whether it is by design or by accident, but you are continually making allusions which— (*aside*) But *she* couldn't know anything.

Fanny. I'm sorry I bungle the matter so, but I'll endeavor to come to the point in as few words as possible.

Merv. If you please. The fewer the better. (*sits again*)

Fanny. If Tom *has* married—Mr. Gilroy I mean—the money's *yours*, and you can retrieve your position without the slightest difficulty.

Merv. (*rising, indignantly*) Take Tom's money ! Blight the prospects of as good a lad as ever lived ! If he *has* married— poor boy ! (although he might have told me) why, all the more reason he should have his money, and I wouldn't touch a shilling of it if I were starving. (*crosses to* L. *corner agitated.*)

Fanny. You really mean that ?

Merv. (*up to her*). Mean it, ha ! ha ! I should think so, and that any woman could have brought herself to make such a pro-position simply amazes me—*amazes* me, Miss Smith, and I *may* add distresses me as well.

Fanny. O, you dear old man !

Merv. What !

Fanny. (*rising*). You dear, darling, nankeenified old love ! I must hug you. (*approaches him.*)

Merv. Go along, ma'am. (*runs up* R. *round table, and behind it in alarm.*)

Fanny. (*follows him to* R. *of table, then sits at his place with comical authority ; points to easy chair* L. *of table*). Sit down. (MERVYN *sits* L. *of table.*)

Fanny. (*taking off her gloves*) Now you stop over there a bit whilst I write. There, I can't write with steel pens, give me *quills ;* they make such a nice noise. (*selects paper, pens &c., and commences writing*)

Merv. (*quite non-plussed ; aside*) That's a remarkable young woman ! She's a genius, or she's mad, or she's something or other remarkable. I'm as rude to her as a man can well be in his own house, and she seems to like me all the better for it. There's some mystery about her. (TOM **enters** *unperceived, from door* L. 2 E.) There's something more than meets the—

Tom. (L. *of* MERVYN) Eye.

Merv. (*looks up, sees* TOM) Oh, *you're* there, sir, eh ?

Tom. Yes ; I'm here, sure enough.

Merv. (*rises, comes* C.) *So,* sir, I've heard a very pretty story about you ! A charming story, Mr. Thomas Gilroy.

Tom. (*coming* L. C.) That's rather odd, for do you know I've just been the recipient of a highly interesting narrative con-cerning *you.*

Merv. (*staggered*) What do you mean by *that,* sir ? If any-one presumes to say anything of *me*, sir, calculated in any way to—to—hang it, Tom, speak out. I've suffered all day from hints and innuendos and vague remarks which—which—what the devil *have* you heard, Thomas Gilroy?

Tom. Ha! ha! ha! what *haven't* I heard!

Merv. *That* I don't care a farthing for. But before you reply, tell me, sir, as your *guardian*, what you meant by getting married and concealing the fact?

Tom. And tell *me*, sir, as your *ward*, what you meant by doing the same.

Merv. (*staggering back, overcome*) How did you know—I mean how did you *guess*—how did—

Tom. There's a sympathy between Benedicks. It's a wonder we never found each other out before.

Merv. Then you are—

Tom. Married? Very much so. And *you?*

Enter MUGGLES *suddenly, door* L. 2 E.

Mug. (L.) Look here, Mr. Gilroy, what's the meaning of all this 'ere? None of your counsellor's airs *here*. Guv'nor, don't you stand no bullying. Mr. Gilroy, you ain't at the Old Bailey, you know.

Tom. (L. C.) No. Take care *you're* not there before you're aware of it. As you've listened at the door, I needn't repeat my remarks. Your master's supposed to be a married man.

Mug. Well, who says he ain't?

Tom. *I* do.

Merv. Tom!

Fanny. Tom, dear!

Mug. Ha! ha! "*Tom, dear.*" " Familirallity breeds *contempt.*" Hem! *Doctor Watts.*

Tom. Ha! Cornwall's a pleasant county, isn't it?

Merv. Eh?

Mug. What?

Tom. Good, secret, retired, out of the way, ostrich-in-the sand, fly-in-the-amber, needle-in-a-bottle-of-hay, toad-in-the-hole, sort of locality, eh, Muggles? Capital county for concealing yourself from your creditors, sort of place where you can live and die without causing any particular remark, first rate place for human flowers to be "born, and blush unseen," for "mute inglorious Miltons, etc., etc.; and above all other advantages a specially admirable neighborhood wherein to *hide a wife.*

Fanny. Eh?

Merv. (*aside*) Oh, law! (*goes up, sits* L. *of table*)

Mug. Well, if *I* had a wife as wanted a hiding, I shouldn't be partick'ler as to the *neighborhood.*

Fanny. (*rises and comes forward* R. C.) But, Tom, what does all this mean?

Mug. (*blusteringly*) I tell you what it means. Mr. Gilroy thinks he's got 'old of something.

Tom. Something and *somebody*. (FANNY *sits again up* R. C.)

Mug. Eh ?

Merv. Some—somebody, Tom ?

Tom. Mr. Muggles, did you ever hear of a party of the name of—a—name of *Goppinger ?*

Mug. (*staggering, aside*) It *was* 'im. I took him for a *loosifer naturee*, but it was *'im*, and there's nothing - for it now but bluster. (*aloud*) He—hem ! Ya—ah, I knew a vagabond of that name. He was transported for a forgery, and—and—

Tom. Has returned.

Enter *from door* L. 2 E., GOPPINGER, *a scrubby, grubby, gray muzzled old man, with bent back, and general appearance of dilapidation, a lawyer's blue bag in his hand. He comes slowly* R. *of* TOM—MUGGLES *being on* TOM'S L.

Merv. Goppinger ? Goppinger ? I never heard the name.

Tom. That's remarkable, considering you married his wife.

Merv. What, sir ?

Fanny. Tom, dear !

Mug. (*with a strong effort to master his alarm*) Ha ! ha ! we're a having a lark, *we* are. Mr. Mervyn, my master here, suttingly did marry, and I'm prepared to swear as he—(*sees* GOPPINGER, *who is now down* R. *of* TOM. *Picture*) Hottiwell Goppinger !

Gop. The werry identical flute.

Mug. Why ain't you in Australia ?

Gop. Why ain't *you ?*

Mug. It's the land of your retreat—leastways your adoption.

Gop. Gove'nment thinks I'm old enough to leave *off* being adopted, and as I ain't killed no warders, though opportoonities was noomerous and irritation continooal, and conducted myself in general first class, why, I've got my ticket of leave. Next time I visits the colonies, David Muggles, (*with concentrated fierceness*), it won't be for *forgery*, and it won't be on your *evidence*, old pal. (*threatens* MUGGLES. TOM *puts him back*. MERVYN *rises and comes forward* C.) He turned agin me, but you won't do so *again*, Davy. So, no sooner was my back turned, and you thought my cough was a settler, than you egged on your soft 'arted guv'nor here to marry my wife, eh, Davy Muggles, eh ? (*half rushing at him.*)

Merv. (*excitedly*, R. C.) What do you say, man ? Do you mean to say that *you—you—*

Tom. Ha ! ha ! ha ! Goppinger isn't inviting to *look* at, but he's—

Merv. I should think he *was.* (*shakes* GOPPINGER *by the hand*) Go on, my dear sir, go on.

Gop. (*to* MERVYN) David there knew when you married buxom Kitty Larchmore, as her real name was Goppinger, and her 'usband living at the time. Fact was he knew you was as soft as—

Merv. That'll do, sir, that'll do. (GOPPINGER *goes up and crosses to* L. *near door; to* MUGGLES) So the shameful thraldom in which you have held me all these years, you ungrateful scoundrel—(*crosses to* C., *to* TOM.) I *may* call him a scoundrel, eh, Tom ?

Tom. No ; you mayn't, but I should.

Merv. Was simply—simply—(*goes and sits* L. *of table.*)

Mug. Cease wituperation. I'm not wanted here, so I shall—

Tom. Before you go you'll give up your books and account for no end of things, Mr. Muggles. This gentleman here was the mysterious correspondent who cautioned me to keep my eye on Muggles, *he's* been doing so for some time ; you see it's a little matter of revenge with him.

Mug. All my fond 'opes vanished. The " Dog and Duck," the private *h*aspiration of years kollopsed—turned, as the poet haves it, " into thin *h*air, and what seemed like a corporal, melted." Hem ! Bard of Evans.

Gop. (L.) Come along, old pal. I'll look after you. I'll *never* leave you. (GOPPINGER *links him with his arm, and leads him, sticking close to him.* MUGGLES' *legs limp, and his general appearance is crestfallen. At the door he turns, but catching* TOM'S *eye—as in* ACT I.—*collapses, and* exeunt *door* L. 2 E.)

Merv. I can scarcely believe my eyes and ears, and I—

Enter PRISCILLA, EMILY *and* ERNEST *quickly from door* R. 2 E.

Pris. (R. C.) What is this ? Miss Smith not gone yet ?

Fanny. (*rises and comes down* C.) No. And strange as it may appear, Miss Smith doesn't mean to go. Emily, dear—

Emily. (R. *corner*) Shameless young woman, don't *look* at me.

Pris. Learn, young woman, that the object of your indelicate attacks is *not* the catch you imagined. He is ruined.

Fanny. Possibly *I* may be able to avert the calamity. *I* possess a little property.

Tom. (*aside*) Halloa !

Emily. Keep it, madam. We'll all starve together rather than owe anything to a person who—who—

Fanny. Gracious me ! what have I done so dreadful ? Mayn't a wife embrace her husband ? (MERVYN *rises and comes down* L.)

Emily. Don't know. I never had one. Besides, poor old dear, he's not your husband *yet.*

Fanny. Explanations are tedious things, but sometimes indispensable. Hear! (*oracularly*) Once on a time—

Merv. |
Pris. | Oh, law!

Fanny. (*resolutely*) Once on a time—

Tom. (L. C.) That's *twice* on a time—go on.

Fanny. (*goes to* TOM) You're more used to this sort of thing, so perhaps *you* will—(*sits up* L. C. MERVYN *seated down* L. PRISCILLA *at* R. *corner of table.* EMILY *next to her.* ERNEST R.)

Tom. (*goes at back of chair* L. *of table in a barrister fashion*) It seems, my lud, that a certain relative of the plaintiff left a somewhat ridiculous clause in his will, forbidding his heir to marry before a certain age, without an elderly relative's consent. The heir in question *did* marry.

Pris. (*excited*) No! Impossible! It's not the fact! I—

Fanny. (*rising in the manner of the court usher*) Si-lence. (*sits again.*)

Tom. But concealed the fact; and after having separated from his wife on a question of wounded pride, being naturally a—a—

Fanny. Obstinate.

Tom. I'm obliged to my learned friend for the adjective—"obstinate" but they met by accident five years after at the house of the elderly relative in question.

Merv. What!

Pris. Thomas!

Emily. Tom!

Fanny. (*rises, comes forward a little, with legal air*) A—Brother Gilroy will permit me to add that the wife, feeling her property an encumbrance (*seriously*) and a bar to her domestic happiness, wrote only this very day, in fact less than half an hour back, to her man of business in London, instructing him to sell out everything without delay, and place the entire sum realized at the disposal of her new found cousin, Mr. Mervyn, (*comes and takes* MERVYN'S *hand, then back to* TOM), so that her husband may come back to her without the slightest pang of wounded pride, and with the knowledge that it will be upon *his* industry, his talent and *success*, that she in future must most properly depend. (*gives* TOM *her hand.*)

Tom. My darling!

Pris. (*comes down* R. C.) Emily, we've been making fools of ourselves. (*goes up and gets round to* L. C.)

Emily. (*coming* R. C.) Oh, Fanny dear, do please forgive me. You know appearances were so much against you. I thought you were fond of Ernest, and that would have been so very dreadful.

Fanny. Yes, it would.

Ernest. Thank you.

Merv. (*to* TOM) But I'm in the clouds. (*puts chair* L.)

Tom. Keep there till we've settled your affairs for you.

Merv. I can't take *her* money. I—

Tom. It *was* hers, then it was mine, and now it's *yours*.

Merv. Never !

Tom. Then you part a loving couple once again. Fanny, farewell forever. (*going* L.)

Merv. (*stopping him*) No, no ; stop, you impetuous fellow.

Fanny. As we can never be re-united, Tom, good-bye, everybody. (*going* R.)

Emily. (*stopping her*) If you go, I'll—I'll never marry Ernest.

Ernest. (*crosses to* R. C.) Oh, hang it, don't go.

Merv. I don't understand it all, but I'm in your hands. And Fanny here—

Tom. (*embracing her*) She's in my *arms*.

Fanny. Oh, Tom.

Ernest. (*embracing* EMILY) There, I can't help it !

Emily. (R.) How *can* you ?

Merv. Confound it, boys, let it go round. (*embraces* PRISCILLA)

Pris. It's all a mystery.

Tom.   I'll make it clear.

But first to solve a greater mystery here. (*indicating audience*)

Our partnership for life again commences,

We come on you, though, for the law expenses

Paid thus—by note of hand—your answer ? Yes.

Then we may count our future a success.

PICTURE.

FANNY.   TOM.

PRISCILLA.   EMILY.

MERVYN.   ERNEST.

CURTAIN.

UNCLE TOM'S CABIN (NEW VERSION.)

A MELODRAMA IN FIVE ACTS, BY CHAS. TOWNSEND.

PRICE, 15 CENTS.

Seven male, five female characters (some of the characters play two parts). Time of playing, 2¼ hours. This is a new acting edition of a prime old favorite, so simplified in the stage-setting as to be easily represented by dramatic clubs and travelling companies with limited scenery. UNCLE TOM'S CABIN is a play that never grows old; being pure and faultless, it commands the praise of the pulpit and support of the press, while it enlists the favor of all Christians and heads of families. It will draw hundreds where other plays draw dozens, and therefore is sure to fill any hall.

SYNOPSIS OF INCIDENTS: ACT I.—*Scene I.*—The Shelby plantation in Kentucky.—George and Eliza.—The curse of Slavery.—The resolve.—Off for Canada.—"I won't be taken—I'll die first."—Shelby and Haley.—Uncle Tom and Harry must be sold.—The poor mother.—"Sell my boy!"—The faithful slave. *Scene II.*—Gumption Cute.—"By Gum!"—Marks, the lawyer.—A mad Yankee.—George in disguise.—A friend in need.—The human bloodhounds.—The escape.—"Hooray fer old Varmount!"

ACT II.—St. Clare's elegant home.—The fretful wife.—The arrival.—Little Eva.—Aunt Ophelia and Topsy.—"O, Golly! I'se so wicked!"—St. Clare's opinion.—"Benighted innocence."—The stolen gloves.—Topsy in her glory.

ACT III.—The angel child.—Tom and St. Clare.—Topsy's mischief.—Eva's request.—The promise.—pathetic scene.—Death of Eva.—St. Clare's grief.—"For thou art gone forever."

ACT IV.—The lonely house.—Tom and St. Clare.—Topsy's keepsake.—Deacon Perry and Aunt Ophelia.—Cute on deck.—A distant relative.—The hungry visitor.—Chuck full of emptiness."—Cute and the Deacon.—A row.—A fight.—Topsy to the rescue.—St. Clare wounded.— Death of St. Clare.—"Eva—Eva—I am coming."

ACT V.—Legree's plantation on the Red River.—Home again.—Uncle Tom's noble heart.—"My soul ain't yours, Mas'r."—Legree's cruel work.—Legree and Cassy.—The white slave.—A frightened brute.—Legree's fear.—A life of sin.—Marks and Cute.—A new scheme.—The dreadful whipping of Uncle Tom.—Legree punished at last.—Death of Uncle Tom.—Eva in Heaven.

THE WOVEN WEB.

A DRAMA IN FOUR ACTS, BY CHAS. TOWNSEND.

PRICE, 15 CENTS.

Seven male, three female characters, viz.: leading and second juvenile men, society villain, walking gentleman, eccentric comedian, old man, low comedian, leading juvenile lady, soubrette and old woman. Time of playing, 2¼ hours. THE WOVEN WEB is a flawless drama, pure in thought and action, with excellent characters, and presenting no difficulties in costumes or scenery. The story is captivating, with a plot of the most intense and unflagging interest, rising to a natural climax of wonderful power. The wit is bright and sparkling, the action terse, sharp and rapid. In touching the great chord of human sympathy, the author has expended that rare skill which has given life to every great play known to the stage. This play has been produced under the author's management with marked success, and will prove an unquestionable attraction wherever presented.

SYNOPSIS OF INCIDENTS: ACT I.—Parkhurst & Manning's law office, New York.—Tim's opinion.—The young lawyer.—"Majah Billy Toby, sah!"—Love and law.—Bright prospects.—Bertha's mi fortune.—A false friend.—The will destroyed.—A cunning plot.—Weaving the web.—The unseen witness.—The letter.—Accused.—Dishonored.

ACT II.—Winter quarters.—Colonel Hastings and Sergeant Tim.—Moses.—A message.—Tim on his dignity.—The arrival.—Playing soldier.—The secret.—The promise.—Harry in danger.—Love and duty.—The promise kept.—"Saved, at the loss of my own honor!"

ACT III.—Drawing-room at Falconer's.—Reading the news.—"Apply to Judy!"—Louise's romance.—Important news.—Bertha's fears.—Leamington's arrival.—Drawing the web.—Threatened.—Plotting.—Harry and Bertha.—A fiendish lie.—Face to face.—"Do you know him?"—Denounced.—"Your life shall be the penalty!"—Startling tableau.

ACT IV.—At Uncle Toby's.—A wonderful climate.—An impudent rascal.— A bit of history.—Woman's wit.—Toby Indignant.—A quarrel.—Uncle Toby's evidence.—Leamington's last trump.—Good news.—Checkmated.—The telegram.—Breaking the web.—Sunshine at last.

☛ *Copies mailed, postpaid, to any address, on receipt of the annexed prices.* ☚

SAVED FROM THE WRECK.

A DRAMA IN THREE ACTS, BY THOMAS K. SERRANO.

PRICE, 15 CENTS.

Eight male, three female characters: Leading comedy, juvenile man, genteel villain, rough villain, light comedy, escaped convict, detective, utility, juvenile lady, leading comedy lady and old woman. Two interior and one landscape scenes. Modern costumes. Time of playing, two hours and a half. The scene of the action is laid on the New Jersey coast. The plot is of absorbing interest, the "business" effective, and the ingenious contrasts of comic and serious situations present a continuous series of surprises for the spectators, whose interest is increasingly maintained up to the final tableau.

SYNOPSIS OF INCIDENTS.

ACT I. THE HOME OF THE LIGHT-HOUSE KEEPER.—An autumn afternoon.—The insult.—True to herself.—A fearless heart.—The unwelcome guest.—Only a foundling.—An abuse of confidence.—The new partner.—The compact.—The dead brought to life.—Saved from the wreck.—Legal advice.—Married for money.—A golden chance.—The intercepted letter.—A vision of wealth.—The forgery.—Within an inch of his life.—The rescue.—TABLEAU.

ACT II. SCENE AS BEFORE; time, night.—Dark clouds gathering.—Changing the jackets.—Father and son.—On duty.—A struggle for fortune.—Loved for himself.—The divided greenbacks.—The agreement.—An unhappy life.—The detective's mistake.—Arrested.—Mistaken identity.—The likeness again.—On the right track —The accident.—"Will she be saved?"—Latour's bravery.—A noble sacrifice.—The secret meeting.—Another case of mistaken identity.—The murder.—"Who did it?"—The torn cuff.—"There stands the murderer!"—"'Tis false!"—The wrong man murdered.—Who was the victim?—TABLEAU.

ACT III. Two DAYS LATER.—Plot and counterplot.—Gentleman and convict.—The price of her life.—Some new documents.—The divided banknotes.—Sunshine through the clouds.—Prepared for a watery grave —Deadly peril —Father and daughter.—The rising tide.—A life for a signature.—True unto death.—Saved.—The mystery solved.—Dénouement.—TABLEAU.

BETWEEN TWO FIRES.

A COMEDY-DRAMA IN THREE ACTS, BY THOMAS K. SERRANO.

PRICE, 15 CENTS.

Eight male, three female, and utility characters: Leading juvenile man, first and second walking gentleman, two light comedians (lawyer and foreign adventurer), Dutch and Irish character comedians, villain, soldiers; leading juvenile lady, walking lady and comedienne. Three interior scenes; modern and military costumes. Time of playing, two hours and a half. Apart from unusual interest of plot and skill of construction, the play affords an opportunity of representing the progress of a real battle in the distance (though this is not necessary to the action). The comedy business is delicious, if well worked up, and a startling phase of the slavery question is sprung upon the audience in the last act.

SYNOPSIS OF INCIDENTS.

ACT I. AT FORT LEE, ON THE HUDSON.—News from the war.—The meeting.—The colonel's strange romance.—Departing for the war.—The intrusted packet.—An honest man.—A last request.—Bitter hatred.—The dawn of love.—A northerner's sympathy for the South.—Is he a traitor?—Held in trust.—La Creole mine for sale.—Financial agents.—A brother's wrong.—An order to cross the enemy's lines.—Fortune's fool.—Love's penalty.—Man's independence.—Strange disclosures.—A shadowed life.—Beggared in pocket, and bankrupt in love.—His last chance.—The refusal.—Turned from home.—Alone, without a name —Off to the war.—TABLEAU.

ACT II. ON THE BATTLEFIELD.—An Irishman's philosophy.—Unconscious of danger.—Spies in the camp.—The insult.—Risen from the ranks.—The colonel's prejudice.—Letters from home.—The plot to ruin.—A token of love.—True to him.—The plotters at work.—Breaking the seals.—The meeting of husband and wife.—A forlorn hope.—Doomed as a spy.—A struggle for lost honor.—A soldier's death.—TABLEAU.

ACT III. BEFORE RICHMOND.—The home of Mrs. De Mori.—The two documents.—A little misunderstanding.—A deserted wife.—The truth revealed.—Brought to light.—Mother and child.—Rowena's sacrifice.—The American Eagle spreads his wings.—The spider's web.—True to himself.—The reconciliation.—A long divided home reunited.—The close of the war.—TABLEAU.

Copies mailed, postpaid, to any address, on receipt of the annexed prices.

NEW ENTERTAINMENTS.

THE JAPANESE WEDDING.

A costume pantomime representation of the Wedding Ceremony in Japanese high life. The company consists of the bride and groom, their parents, six bridesmaids, and the officiating personage appropriately called the "Go-between." There are various formalities, including salaams, tea-drinking, eating rice-cakes, and giving presents. No words are spoken. The ceremony (which occupies about 50 minutes), with the "tea-room," fills out an evening well, though music and other attractions may be added. Can be represented by young ladies alone, if preferred. **Price, 25 Cents.**

AN EVENING WITH PICKWICK.

A Literary and Dramatic Dickens Entertainment.—Introduces the Pickwick Club, the Wardles of Dingley Dell, the Fat Boy, Alfred Jingle, Mrs. Leo Hunter, Lord Mutanhed and Count Smorltork, Arabella Allen and Bob Allen, Bob Sawyer, Mrs. and Master Bardell, Mrs. Cluppins, Mrs. Weller, Stiggins, Tony Weller, Sam Weller, and the Lady Traveller. **Price, 25 cents.**

AN EVENING WITH COPPERFIELD.

A Literary and Dramatic Dickens Entertainment.—Introduces Mrs. Copperfield, Davie, the Peggotys, the Murdstones, Mrs. Gummidge, Little Em'ly, Barkis, Betsey Trotwood, Mr. Dick and his kite, Steerforth, the Creakles, Traddles, Rosa Dartle, Miss Mowcher, Uriah Heep and his Mother, the Micawbers, Dora and Gyp, and the wooden-legged Gatekeeper. **Price, 25 cents.**

These "Evenings with Dickens" can be represented in whole or in part, require but little memorizing, do not demand experienced actors, are not troublesome to prepare, and are suitable for performance either on the platform or in the drawing room.

THE GYPSIES' FESTIVAL.

A Musical Entertainment for Young People. Introduces the Gypsy Queen, Fortune Teller, Yankee Peddler, and a Chorus of Gypsies, of any desired number. The scene is supposed to be a Gypsy Camp. The costumes are very pretty, but simple; the dialogue bright; the music easy and tuneful; and the drill movements and calisthenics are graceful. Few properties and no set scenery required, so that the entertainment can be represented on any platform. **Price, 25 cents.**

THE COURT OF KING CHRISTMAS.

A CHRISTMAS ENTERTAINMENT. The action takes place in Santa Claus land on Christmas eve, and represents the bustling preparations of St. Nick and his attendant worthies for the gratification of all children the next day. The cast may include as many as 36 characters, though fewer will answer, and the entertainment represented on a platform, without troublesome properties. The costumes are simple, the incidental music and drill movements graceful and easily managed, the dialogue uncommonly good, and the whole thing quite above the average. A representation of this entertainment will cause the young folks, from six to sixty, fairly to turn themselves inside out with delight, and, at the same time, enforce the important moral of Peace and Good Will. **Price, 25 cents.**

RECENTLY PUBLISHED.

ILLUSTRATED TABLEAUX FOR AMATEURS. A new series of *Tableaux Vivants*, by MARTHA C. WELD. In this series each description is accompanied with a full-page illustration of the scene to be represented.
PART I.—MISCELLANEOUS TABLEAUX.—Contains General Introduction, 12 Tableaux and 14 Illustrations. **Price, 25 Cents.**
PART II.—MISCELLANEOUS TABLEAUX.—Contains Introduction, 12 Tableaux and 12 illustrations. **Price, 25 Cents.**
SAVED FROM THE WRECK. A drama in three acts. Eight male, three female characters. Time, two hours and a half. **Price, 15 Cents.**
BETWEEN TWO FIRES. A comedy-drama in three acts. Eight male, three female characters. Time, two hours and a half. **Price, 15 Cents.**
BY FORCE OF IMPULSE. A drama in five acts. Nine male, three female characters. Time, two hours and a half. **Price, 15 Cents.**
A LESSON IN ELEGANCE. A comedy in one act. Four female characters. Time, thirty minutes. **Price, 15 Cents.**
WANTED, A CONFIDENTIAL CLERK. A farce in one act. Six male characters. Time, thirty minutes. **Price, 15 Cents.**
SECOND SIGHT. A farcical comedy in one act. Four male, one female character. Time, one hour. **Price, 15 Cents.**
THE TRIPLE WEDDING. A drama in three acts. Four male, four female characters. Time, one hour and a quarter. **Price, 15 cents.**

☞ *Any of the above will be sent by mail, postpaid, to any address, on receipt of the annexed prices.* ☜

HAROLD ROORBACH, Publisher, 9 Murray St., New York.

HELME
ACTOR'S MAKE

0 014 458 603 7

A Practical and Systematic Guide to the Art of Making up for the Stage.

PRICE, 25 CENTS.

WITH EXHAUSTIVE TREATMENT ON THE USE OF THEATRICAL WIGS AND BEARDS, THE MAKE-UP AND ITS REQUISITE MATERIALS, THE DIFFERENT FEATURES AND THEIR MANAGEMENT, TYPICAL CHARACTER MASKS, ETC. WITH SPECIAL HINTS TO LADIES. DESIGNED FOR THE USE OF ACTORS AND AMATEURS, AND FOR BOTH LADIES AND GENTLEMEN. COPIOUSLY ILLUSTRATED.

CONTENTS.

Sent by mail, postpaid, to any address, on receipt of the price.

HAROLD ROORBACH, Publisher,
9 Murray Street, New York.